Lisa

A Private Event

Gillian Garnham

Published by Biscuit Publishing Ltd. 2005

Copyright © Gillian Garnham 2005

ISBN 1-903914-21-3

The right of Gillian Garnham to be identified as the author of this book has been asserted by her in accordance with the Copyright, Designs and Patents Act 1988

All of the characters in this book are fictitious, and any resemblance to actual persons, living or dead, is purely coincidental.

A catalogue for this book is available from the British Library.

First published in Great Britain by
Biscuit Publishing Ltd., 2005
PO Box 123, Washington
Newcastle upon Tyne
NE37 2YW

Typeset by Mike Wilson, Bridlington

Front cover design by James Cianciaruso © 2005

Printed and bound in Great Britain by
Jasprint Ltd., Tyne & Wear

"I first became aware of Gillian Garnham's ability to create atmosphere when I read her (prize-winning) story *A Place Proper to Grow Wise in*. Here, she has done it again. In *A Private Event* you will see, taste and hear Paris in the Sixties and be gripped by a tale of love and loss, betrayal and loyalty set against the background of social unrest and the violent Paris riots. I defy you, once you have begun this book, to put it down." **Denise Robertson**

"A time of change, of political and social agitation, a period of uncertainty when people and events are never quite as they seem. Ella seeks to make sense of it all in this beautifully crafted and exquisitely written novel."
Patrick Conway

"It [*A Private Event*] reveals a France of secrets, betrayals a France noir . . . village with its own peasant dark powers . . . source of brutal passion and lust. The book is intense, pacy, deeply imagined." **Michael Standen**

"Gillian Garnham takes the 1968 Paris riots out of the realm of cinematic stills or journalistic footage and into a less stylised domestic arena, fraught with the drama and tensions of ordinary people. Reading *A Private Event* is an experience as vivid and unexpected as catching a goldfish falling from the sky." **Crista Ermiya**

"The style of prose is masterful . . . evocation of place and acceptance of affairs of the heart insinuate from the pages. This beautifully written book . . . evokes a time and a place to draw the reader in . . . deserves a place in everyone's mind." **Ruth Henderson**

"Observing a writer hit their stride is a real thrill. Gillian Garnham is up and running with a wonderfully atmospheric novel that deserves accolades . . . tightly woven study of love and betrayal set against a background of rising violence. A riveting read from start to finish." **Alison Lister**

For Barry

A Private Event

Gillian Garnham

I

It caught the sun – as it fell – and he caught it in his cupped hands.
A goldfish falling out of the sky.
'*Hop-là!*' He saw it coming, and took a dive across the crazy paving. Caught it. 'Wheeeeeow!' – and in through the back door, up the steps, three at a time, through the bedroom and onto the balcony to plop it back into its tank on the stone balustrade.
In the garden below, the girl was raking into piles the old leaves left lying from last autumn. 'Is it alive?' She paused in her sweeping. 'Is it swimming?' She pressed the fingers of one hand over her mouth, as if holding her breath.
And he, peering into the water and swirling it round with his finger, cried – 'Yes! Ah ...? Yes, it's okay!' and then a roar of laughter. 'I caught it! Jesus! You saw me!' He leant over the balustrade, his arms outstretched towards her.
'Oh you!' she said. 'Mad. Mad!' but she laughed up at him.
He gave the water another swirl, and turned back into the bedroom. The long voile curtains, off-white, more grey than white, breathed in and out in the chill breeze.
The leaves were wet and they stuck to the girl's shoes, so that every now and then she paused to peel them off. The last night's frost was melting in the fresh March sun, but the over-grown garden, for too long disregarded, still had that dank smell of winter upon it.
When the woman came out of the bedroom to inspect the fish, he was right behind her, telling her how he had caught it. The girl below kept her eyes on the brown leaves, but she could see the two of them, with their heads together as they looked into the small, square tank. It was

her fish – the woman's – and it was called Albertine. What a name for a fish, thought the girl. The woman's name was Madame Madeleine Tessier. She was tall, but looked no more than average height beside the exceptionally tall man; he was well over six foot, and had that slight stoop of those with a willowy frame who had been unable to stop growing. As if their slender bodies only just managed to support the height. He was dark, black as black his hair, which fell over his eyes like a thick mat. A 'glib' they call it in Ireland, that mass of hair over the eyes. At his age, somewhere around his middle forties, even older, the young girl would have expected it to be going grey, and indeed there were little touches of grey to left and right temple, but it was hardly anything, and the black glib was so heavy that it was only if you were close, very close indeed, and able to lift the fringe with a finger, that you would be able to see those tell-tale scratches of silver. Where his hair was dark, the woman's was blonde, but the roots were black, at a time when it was not at all fashionable to show its so obviously bottled origin. When Madeleine used the new bathroom, she remained there for hours, and left behind a trail of mauve stains upon the floor, smudges on the towels, the basin, the brand new bath tub, which this English girl, Ella, had to scrub clean. Once a month (or longer) the sharp smell of peroxide filled the house. Now, with the cloak of sleep still on her, and her hair unbrushed, the stiff yellow tufts sat on her head like a crown.

'Did he catch it? Did it jump out?' She was resting her hands on the balustrade and leaning over to shout down to the girl. Then she dropped her voice, so that Ella had to leave her piles of leaves and step closer to the house, and tilt her face up to the woman to hear what she was saying. A drop of water landed on her cheek. It would have been from the melting frost, as the sun touched the round stone balustrade, but she felt it as a drop of spittle from Madeleine's tongue, and she wiped it away with the back of her hand.

'Is he teasing me?' – in a conspiratorial whisper, and leaning over a little further. 'I can't believe it. What a naughty man!' She turned to him, and ran a finger down over his nose, as one might an animal. 'That you just happened to be there! *Méchant!* And it jumped into your hands? Just like that! Extraordinary! But I don't believe it. No. Not for a minute.'

The two of them turned back into the bedroom. He following, with his long arms flailing and his voice raised as he excitedly asserted the veracity of his tale.

For it was true. Really. Incredible as it sounds, he did catch it. He caught a fish alive-alive-o. On that spring morning in 1968. Early in the morning (but not too early because Madeleine always slept late), he had been looking up at her window and a shining fish had come swimming down through the sky. Like a sunbeam. Like a falling star.

The tall man was Charles Fontenay. He lived barely a hundred yards away, further down the hill which led up to the house; the road continued on until it reached the edge of the forest. The village, Montesson-la-Forêt, at the foot of the hill, close to the Seine, at a point where the river was thin and a bit straggly, provided the usual shops – *Boulangerie, Epicerie, Boucherie, Pharmacie* – and there was the regular Sunday market in the square next to the railway station. The station itself provided an easy journey into Paris: exactly twenty-four minutes – for the trains ran strictly to time and the slightest of delays prompted immediate complaints. A small village on the outskirts of Paris, with not much of a claim to fame, other than the hairdresser down near the station, who had been the lover of Edith Piaf. It was the sort of place where a little gossip went a long way. Whatever the interest in the hairdresser (and its list of clients had significantly increased since the spread of the story of his love), Charles Fontenay was its more famous resident. As a writer of popular fiction, he was not to be called a master of letters – that honour was reserved for Madeleine's husband, *Le*

Professeur – but he was a man to be indulged. If he hadn't paid his bills, well that was alright. Monsieur Fontenay might need to be nudged rather more frequently than the individual shopkeepers and business owners would have liked – 'after all Monsieur, we all have a living to make,' polite laughter – but they put it down to the absent-mindedness of a writer, and in the end they always got their money and knew that a man of his standing was unlikely to do a runner. All were familiar with his house, its huge gates and thick hedge, and most were not a little proud of his (and by association their) success. There was no bookshop here, but they could see his novels prominently displayed in Paris. They recognized their village and its environs in many of the stories, and they occasionally recognized their neighbours; sometimes, although this could be rather less agreeable, they even saw themselves! Charles Fontenay had become a publisher's dream and his regular supply of middlebrow novels rarely failed to sell.

This dependability sat oddly with his more eccentric personality. His writing seemed to provide the steadying ballast he needed; without it, he said, his life would have continued the aimless drifting of his youth. He had never married and never openly admitted to any children, although on this question he habitually tapped his nose and suggested that possibly not a few were scattered across the country – 'Across the world, my friend. Who knows?' But most people felt that they did know. Charles had an eye for the ladies, but was, some said, a little too much of a lady himself.

It seems that his relationship with Madeleine was not unlike that which he had with his writing. It too gave him security and a harbour of sorts. He liked the life of the solitary writer, but he also liked the uncommitted life of a confidant in her household. She liked to talk to him and found him endlessly amusing. It provided for him a sort of family life, but one in which he remained free to do as he chose. He could visit if he was in need of companionship, but he did not feel committed to do so. If he did not wish to stay for dinner, he was not obliged to. If he wanted to turn up for breakfast, usually after Madeleine's husband, Alain, had departed for the University at Nanterre, no one minded, least of all Madeleine. He frequently breakfasted with her in her bedroom – in the summer, on the balcony, in full view of the village. Nobody, and certainly nobody who had lived there for any length of time, would have called this arrangement an affair or an escapade, although it was open to all to see that they enjoyed each other's company.

'There are two hearts,' said the butcher. 'One belongs in the trousers and the other ...,' he would sigh and place his hand upon the left side of his jacket (where, in fact, he kept his wallet, but on this occasion that was not the intended implication), 'well, my friend, the other is ... that is altogether something else – *tout à fait autre chose*.'

As for her husband, Alain, this friendship with his wife appeared to be of no consequence, in part, no doubt, because he and Charles had a relationship of their own. The friendship between the two men was not altogether unlike that between Charles and Madeleine, for there was that similar mix of closeness and distance. It seemed as if the marriage barrier, which acted as something of a protective shield for Madeleine, was used by Alain and Charles for much the same reason. It allowed a relaxed camaraderie: they went hunting together in the forests nearby, and they usually ended up at the bar in one of the villages, laughing over a glass of wine – but it allowed another less obvious friendship, one which was not overtly acknowledged. This friendship was like the weeds in a river, growing deep down beneath the surface of the water, drifting with the current, now and again visible, but only if the river was low and the water clear; most often it remained hidden. At least, that was how it appeared to the English girl, Ella, and she was the one who was most closely involved in the delicacies of these relationships – apart, that is, from Madame Vinelli, of course.

The house was called *La Fauvette* – the little singing bird: it was named after Madeleine's mother, Madame Vinelli, who still owned and lived in it, and when younger had had a beautiful singing voice – 'Like a lark,' they used to say, 'she sings like a lark.' It was also said that her husband had called her '*ma petite fauvette*' and that it was he who had been responsible for transferring this term of endearment to the house itself. Madame Vinelli now occupied only the ground floor (although Ella, the English girl, slept on that same floor with the two-year-old, Sissy). The upper floor had been given over to her daughter, Madeleine, and her husband, Alain, when they'd married. Madame Vinelli's rooms were furnished in faded Louis Quinze style, and the shutters, winter and summer alike, were closed against the daylight, only to be opened on Sundays, day of rest and the local market, and also on feast days. Shortage of money necessitated her working at a nine to five job in Paris. Her son-in-law paid a small amount in rent. Nobody attended church, although a plaster Madonna and a Saint Theresa stood on a small table near the unused door at the back of the house. Saint Theresa had lost her nose and the Madonna had a few fingers of her right hand missing, as well as a bit from the end of her chin.

It was a house which had seen better days. It must once have been quite imposing, but then, 1968, it was falling into a sulky decay. Like an old lady who had let herself go, it had turned its back upon the world and that back gave onto the muddy lane: rue J-J Rousseau. Barely a road and not really deserving of its elevated title, it had deteriorated to little better than a pot-holed pathway. What had once been the front of the house, with its balcony, balustrades and portico, looked down into the garden and beyond that to the butcher's house and shop. The butcher himself observed the occupants of the house through binoculars. For him Madeleine was worth watching and someone who deserved the carefully trimmed *filets de boeuf* which he supplied each Saturday, wrapping them carefully with his hairless, blood-stained hands: it was a disappointment to him if the girl, Ella, went down to collect the meat. This foreign girl was pretty enough, but not quite up to Madame Tessier's style. He would send out his young son to serve her, without bothering to wrap the meat himself:

'Oh, it's the young English girl, is it? You'll find Madame's *filets* at the side of the front tray.'

Possibly, in the distant past, when the house had been in its heyday, the butcher's premises would not have been there at all, and the garden would have followed right down to the road, the road to Paris. The front door at the back, the one with the portico, was rarely used – hardly ever. The autumn leaves gathered on the terracotta tiles in the porch and remained heaped in corners, despite or because of the half-hearted spring sweepings, each year adding more offerings. The rendering on the exterior walls was flaking, as was the plaster and wallpaper inside. This lady of a house was well past her best. It was as if the building had become listless and bored, rather like Madeleine herself, who lay in bed half the morning and wandered around in her dressing-gown until lunch. When her baby was born, it had been early and a light weight. The doctor had not expected it to survive, but it did, and now was a healthy, pretty little girl. When Madeleine had first seen the child, her feelings had only been those of disappointment. She hadn't wanted to feed it and had felt no attachment to the scrawny, red-skinned mite. So Simone, as she was named, later to be familiarly known as Sissy, had been farmed out to an elderly woman who lived up the muddy lane. This woman had acted as midwife at the birth and had agreed to mind the child until, as Madeleine said, she had reached a less damp stage of life. At two and a half years and house-trained, she was moved back into the family home. The English girl, Ella, had more or less tumbled into the family, and without it ever formally being agreed, she had taken over the care of the child for part of the week, in order to ease the pressure on the mother's nerves. Madeleine lived upon her nerves – they said.

On Saturday mornings, round about ten o'clock, one or other of the villagers would be likely to see Charles Fontenay walking with his springing stride up the hill towards *La Fauvette*, carrying a fat envelope in his hand. When he reached his friends' house, he did not necessarily visit, but simply popped or stuffed his envelope (the slit in the box was narrow and he invariably had plenty to say) into the mailbox at the entrance, before returning to his own shrouded property. When the postman passed by with his letters, he would see through the window of the box the familiar cream envelope, addressed in Charles's unmistakable violet ink to Monsieur Alain Tessier, and when Madeleine came to empty the box, she would leave this single letter lying there to be collected later by her husband.

Similarly, on Wednesday mornings, at around eight o'clock, anyone who happened to be watching would see Alain Tessier walk down to the house of Charles Fontenay, clutching a blue, much thinner envelope. He, in his turn, would slide it into the *boîte à lettres*, giving a firm pull on the bell chain to let his friend know that he had called. He then walked back up the hill to collect his car to drive the twenty minutes or so to the University at Nanterre, walking rather stiffly, with his arms by his side. He would drag his feet a little.

Theirs was a literary correspondence. Each kept safely the letters from the other. Those from Alain were piled in an old pillow-case, which Charles kept in the wardrobe of his bedroom, next to the fruit liqueurs. Charles's were more tidily arranged by Alain in a small wooden filing cabinet in the dining-room of *La Fauvette*. Although neither of them would have dreamt of discussing future publication, there was no doubt that each epistle was written with posterity in mind.

Alain, teacher and scholar in political sciences, was also a writer, but in his case, it was academic works and serious fiction. The fiction centred upon the last war, including the complex and delicate subject of his country's wartime collaboration with Germany. This was not altogether a welcome area of enquiry and sales of his books were slim. The single word titles – *Traitor; Treason; Assassin* – indicated the squeezed style of his writing: some might call it mean, but that would be unfair and it would be better to describe it as precise. He had produced a number of these slender volumes, all fixed upon the same themes of war and betrayal. Whereas Charles's works were like a hearty meal, more English than French, with all the vegetables and meat piled up onto one plate and sodden with gravy, Alain's concise little texts were *Nouvelle Cuisine*, leaving the gastronome's taste buds sharpened but not entirely satisfied.

Madeleine was not entirely satisfied either: her marriage to Alain might have sharpened her mind, but her senses remained dulled. The marriage to her university teacher had not exactly brought her the excitement anticipated. She was now barely twenty-five and living still with her mother in the house which they had always occupied. In many ways, things were much the same as they had been before she'd married, the only difference being that her mother had shifted downstairs to the ground floor, and Alain had moved into her bed – and, of course, they'd got the new bathroom. It's true that the arrival of Sissy had been a diversion, but as she'd been a part-time baby, she hadn't really brought major changes to her mother's life. Neighbours may have thought little of Madame Tessier's friendship with their respected novelist, but she thought a good deal of it, indeed she thought of it most of the time and looked forward to his visits – and most especially the night-time ones.

1968 was a busy year, a very busy year, an eventful year, and no more so than for those politically on the left, as was Alain Tessier. There were times when he found himself obliged to stay overnight on a camp bed at the University in Nanterre. It was regrettable, he said to his wife, in his slightly formal way, but the times were troubled ones and demanded much of him. The students were becoming increasingly disruptive: they didn't like this and they didn't like that. They wanted smaller classes; they wanted less lecturing; they wanted more sex; they wanted less parental discipline from those they considered over the hill; they wanted the future and not the past. The style and content of teaching was out-of-date. They were sick to death of the lingering flavour of post-war austerity, and they wanted off with the old and on with the new. They wanted America out of Vietnam.

Angry voices chimed with others round the world, from Washington to Tokyo, and places in between. For them, it was a sort of 'bliss,' to be sure, and to be young, possibly, 'very heaven,' but for those older and more cautious, such as Alain, who wanted to guide, and even to direct their revolt, there were times when their shoutings and bickerings, all their pent-up frustration, risked fragmenting the democratic and anti-imperialistic ideals for which he stood. He was with the students – yes – over many issues, but his natural reticence and scholarly training cautioned him against too hasty a course of action.

As for Madeleine, on certain mornings, when she was sure that the little camp bed in Nanterre was going to be occupied that night, she would listen to his worries over their bowls of coffee and the grilled bread left from the day before, nod her head sagely and wave him off to struggle with ideals and realities. But as soon as decent, she herself would head off down to the Fontenay mailbox with her very own small blue envelope, scented with Chanel No.5. And nobody who saw her thought a thing about it: *'Bonjour Madame'* – off, of course, to post her husband's letter to his dear friend Monsieur Fontenay, home-bred novelist and such a gentleman. Hadn't he cared for his invalid mother right up until her death? Sons like that don't grow on every bush. God bless him.

On entering *La Fauvette* by the back door, sweet singing birds were not really the first things that came to mind. A most foul smell issued from the W.C. immediately on the right: a Water-Closet which actually had no water and therefore no flush mechanism – hence the stench. The evil smell wafted round the ground floor, invading all rooms, sliding into corners, clinging to furnishings like a palpable presence, but its attempt to sneak up the stairs was thwarted by the descending blast of peroxide, bath oils, Chanel No.5 from Madeleine's ablutions. Next to this downstairs waterless closet, a door opened onto a steep flight of stone steps, leading down to a cellar. There was also an exterior entrance to this cellar through a small door in the garden, that, too, at the foot of stone steps. Madeleine was in the habit of leaving open this outside entrance. The door from the cellar into the actual house was never locked, although there were large, rusty bolts on both sides should anyone wish to fasten it.

Some nights, when Ella was lying awake – she was a poor sleeper – she would hear the sound of the catch of the cellar door; only a click, followed by a slight scuffle, but she had sharp ears. The cellar light switch was over by the garden door, and she could imagine this tall, gangly man fumbling in the black across the cellar, up the steep steps and into the dark hallway, to meet the smell from the closet. She thought of him sniffing and wrinkling his nose, before setting off to find his love. If Ella listened very hard indeed, she imagined that she heard the rhythmic creaking of the bedsprings in the marital bed above. And, if she really strained her ears, she thought that she caught a little cry of delight, like a small animal released from a trap. At such times, to be young for Madeleine was also 'very heaven.'

The fish died, of course, as well it might. Out of its

element, its flight, however brief, hadn't altogether agreed with it. Soon it was tilting over, as if all its innards had tipped to one side, and in no time at all it was floating at the top of the tank ready to be flushed down the pan – the one upstairs, of course. Let it have a watery grave! That's the way it was, that day in March 1968, in a small place on the outskirts of Paris, one minute flying, the next ... and that was how this tale began to take shape. The personal was political with a vengeance then, and there was, amongst some, a disinclination to distinguish between private and public life. This story draws breath – and it draws blood – from the wider 'events' as they came to be known – *Les Evénements* – the almost revolution of 1968.

II

Like a falling star, it was, and on that day in March, the day the goldfish leapt, Ella watched the two of them turn back into the bedroom, and she looked down the garden to where the little child, Sissy, was peering through the wire netting at chickens and ducklings, and at a big turkey which had had a Christmas reprieve and been left to fatten for Easter – with no hope of resurrection. His gobbler was bright red.

There was the sound of an engine in the lane at the back, and Ella recognized it as that of Alain Tessier's Citroën, one of those low black cars still around in the nineteen-sixties and now associated with Simenon's Maigret and French 'B' movies of the time. Looked at today, from the high view point of a twenty-first century 4 × 4, these old Citroëns seem sat upon, close to the ground, nosing along, like some primeval reptile. Ella glanced up at the bedroom window, but Charles Fontenay was already outside and waving farewell. He pushed his fat cream envelope into the mailbox and set off down the lane towards the parked car, carefully avoiding the muddy puddles. Alain had opened the driver's door and was struggling to get out of the low seat. He was not a tall man, by any means, and the low chassis seemed to swallow him: he had one foot on the running-board as Charles came level. Ella had gone to watch, and she sensed that Alain would feel at a disadvantage, half-in and half-out, as the other man stooped to shake his hand. She watched Charles bend down to greet his friend, before continuing on down the hill towards his own house close to the station. Alain turned to watch him go, but the frame of the car door blocked his view and he had to lean forward to see those long legs striding homewards.

After he was no longer in sight, Alain sat there for a minute, as if thinking about his friend, but perhaps it was simply weariness that kept him slumped in his seat. He never slept particularly well on the folding bed in his university room: the mattress was too thin, but staying on site also meant that students called round in the evening and all the welcome wine and talk left him feeling agitated and unready for sleep. His mind was crammed with all that he'd left behind to sort out. Just entering the campus, getting a foot in the place, was a hassle these days, with journalists and police milling around, groups of students spreading themselves all over the place, busy daubing banners (he'd had a can of paint spilt over his shoes – splashed up his trousers), passing round the recipe – not for coq au vin but Molotov cocktails! If it wasn't all so bloody serious, there were times when he wanted to laugh. Graffiti about age and sexuality – *Professors you're past it and your days are dead* – made him run a tentative hand over his thinning hair. He'd got to get a grip on things. He stretched into the back of this lowslung car to get his briefcase, a scruffy brown leather one, the handle so worn that the metal showed through, swung his legs round and stepped out into a pile of shit, deposited there by a neighbour's yappy terrier. He swore.

Slamming the door, he stared at his house and it returned the bleak gaze. It wasn't in fact his, as well he knew, and more than that, his mother-in-law made it perfectly clear to him that she thought him a damned nuisance. There were times when he felt no more than a lodger there. She also made it obvious that, whatever he might think and whatever the marriage licence might prove, his wife wasn't altogether his either: well, that was no surprise. He knew what Charles was up to, what worried him was not the fact that he was sharing his wife but that he didn't really care. His mother-in-law, thankfully, was not aware of the *ménage à trois*. Her dislike related to his generally poor marriage credentials; in her view, he had been a meagre catch. It was also none too comforting to know that he was nearer his mother-in-law's age than his wife's, nor that Charles Fontenay (although of similar age), had money, reputation and looks which were altogether more acceptable.

Thoughts of Charles with his mat of black hair made his fingers itch to stroke his own – reassurance, perhaps. As he passed the boot, he instinctively gave the rounded place covering the spare wheel an affectionate pat. Sight of the fat cream envelope in the mailbox focused his thoughts more securely on Charles and away from what the man was up to with his wife. Although there was obviously nothing else there, out of habit, he ran his fingers over the inside of the empty box. His wife appeared at the door, shivering as she pulled a dressing-gown over her shoulders. He thought that she looked as tired as he felt and, in spite of himself, he winced as he acknowledged the probable reason for her exhaustion.

'Has the postman been?' he asked.

'Not yet. It's not even ten. You're back early. Did you get the bread?'

'Ah!' and he swore quietly under his breath. 'I'll go down in a minute.'

'Don't bother. Ella will go. She's round the back with Sissy. Maman's not up yet. And by the way, some of those lads and their Lambrettas were here again yesterday. You know the ones? Are they your students? They were still around when Maman got home last night.' She pressed her lips together. 'She doesn't like them.'

Instead of going into the house, he tucked the envelope into his jacket pocket and went round to the garden, where he found Ella still lethargically sweeping the leaves. Her long hair was drooping over her face. A lovely face, he thought, and that age-old longing resurfaced as a familiar pain.

He cleared his throat to attract her attention. 'Where's Sissy?'

'With the chickens,' she propped the broom against the wall and smiled towards him. He put down his briefcase, feeling quite weak with desire. What a life! But Ella was still talking to him and he tried hard to concentrate on fowl. 'We had five eggs this morning and that white hen's losing all its feathers. Sissy wanted to look at the turkey. It's really angry' – and then – 'The fish jumped out of the tank. Right over the balcony!'

'What?' he couldn't understand what she was talking about.

'The fish – jumped out of the tank.'

'What a clever fish.'

'Monsieur Fontenay caught it.' She cupped her hands by way of explanation.

'Ah! Did he, indeed. Clever bastard! Caught it – what in his hands? Amazing what that man can do!' He threw back his head and laughed much more loudly than he'd intended. Sissy heard him and ran up through the garden towards him. He stretched out his arms to catch her and lifted her up on his shoulders.

'What a big girl you are now – we're like the man on stilts. Remember the circus?' He strode round the garden, taking long strides, deliberately bobbing so that the child bounced up and down.

'Papa! Papa!' she shouted. 'Be a horse' – and he started to run.

'Careful, Sissy,' cried Ella. 'Hang on! Don't fall!'

'Maman! Look at me!'

Ella looked up to her mother's bedroom to see if she was watching. She saw the windows close.

Alain Tessier was very fond of his small daughter, and she had the looks and brightness which had first attracted him to her mother, so few years ago, a young, wide-eyed student. At Sissy's birth, he'd been upset and bewildered when his wife had been so distant towards the child, almost as if she resented her. He couldn't understand it. When she cried, her mother had stared blankly into the cot, as if she barely knew what she was and what she wanted. In his distress, Alain had discussed this strange behaviour with Charles.

'It happens,' said Charles. 'Animals are sometimes like that – just can't seem to want to feed one or all of their pups. The English are a bit like it, too, I believe. They push their young off to live away in boarding schools as soon as they can – nannies and so on.'

Although Alain had known that his friend's version of childcare across the channel was extreme, he nevertheless had nodded, lost in his own concerns over the new baby.

'It's not as if she's far from you – with the old woman,' Charles had continued, seeing Alain's miserable face.

'No. No.'

'You can call in whenever you want, I suppose?'

'Yes, of course. But – I don't know – it's that old biddy's face – the midwife – that's enough to put you off.'

'I suppose it's clean, is it? Her house?'

'Well I hope so. My mother-in-law's supposed to have looked into that side of things.'

'Well, then? Don't worry. Kids survive – as long as they're fed plenty.'

Alain grimaced, finding little solace in his friend's company over these sorts of matters. Understandable, he supposed, since the man had hinted to him that he had fathered many in whom he had not a modicum of interest. He looked sideways at his friend, wondering whether this virility could possibly be true. As for himself, well perhaps his feelings were in part to do with his own upbringing, when he had found his mother's disposition cold. He'd been an only child, quiet and studious, and left overmuch to his own devices. He had hoped that for his own children, and he had always thought of offspring in the plural, things would be different.

He, as a lonely child, became in essence a rather lonely man. He thought it interesting to consider whether enforced and voluntary isolation in childhood could have coloured his later career and political thinking. Solitariness had became a habit and a difficult one to discard or want to discard, but it didn't mean that he didn't long to be part of a group. A longing for comradeship and a fear of comradeship, as if afraid of losing something of the self, he imagined not unusual. Politically and personally, communism had offered him an attractive theory, and he always remembered talking to a Russian defector about the terror this man had experienced when he had arrived in the West, simply, at first, because of the responsibilities thrown upon the individual, ones which he had never had to face before. 'Everything had been decided for me until then,' he'd said. 'Strangely, there is something quite attractive in that, although I cannot espouse it as an admirable solution to social living!'

Alain had listened and had found himself wondering whether it suggested something fundamental in human nature; the always seeking after personal responsibility but often finding that responsibility hard to bear. Behind everyone, he thought, might be the desire, if only now and again, to scurry back to the burrow and let someone else take over. He had even speculated on this with Charles, who had roared with laughter:

'Head in the sand, eh? Is that what you want? Ah, *mon brave!*' But, if he had thought a little, he would have found that such questions were not inappropriate to his own life.

'No, of course not. It's the multiplicity of choice. Wanting to be sure that one's actions are the right ones – are the best for the self and for others.'

'Can't stand by your principles. Is that it?' And then Alain had simply laughed as well, shrugged and regretted his momentary admission of weakness.

In so many ways the two men's personalities might be seen as contrasting: Charles was ebullient and often hasty, where Alain was controlled and thoughtful. Charles was contented to produce what he knew were pot-boilers, but Alain pored over his writings, amending and editing with meticulous care. Alain was drawn towards a personality, seemingly so unlike his own, and watching Charles when out hunting, firing at everything in sight, he found amusing and exhilarating – it was the letting go which he envied. Charles expended a lot of energy, but he was the one who always bagged the prize – and now he'd won his friend's wife. One day Charles had shot a wild boar, a huge grandaddy of a boar, with tusks ... well he had them still, hanging on his bedroom wall.

'They'd have your hand off,' he said. 'Look at the size of them. They work like gigantic scissors. My God!'

As Alain's gallop slowed to a walk, his daughter clutching onto the collar of his jacket (hair not being much of an option), he mulled over this relationship with Charles, thinking that it could be true that individuals are attracted to contrary personalities, but also, and perhaps equally true, that they actively seek after some reflection of themselves, maybe to reinforce their self-understanding or, more crudely, as a means of self-validation? He was beginning to believe that the latter was closer to the truth and that some of what he envied in Charles had been suppressed in himself and was now, a bit late in life – no, in full maturity – that sounded much better – *now* beginning to emerge.

With that warm thought in mind, he glanced at the lovely Ella, and when he was sure that she was looking at him, bent over and tippled Sissy down onto the muddy grass. She rolled over and over in the dirt.

'Sissy!' cried Ella, running towards them both. 'You're getting filthy.'

The child jumped up and ran off towards the house with Alain and Ella in pursuit, and as they ran, he took her hand. She smiled happily up at him. The family cat tumbled down from an apple tree, landed on all four legs, and for a moment stood there shaking itself as if stunned by the fall, then it shot ahead of them. Cat and Sissy hurled themselves through the open door and nearly knocked over Madame Vinelli, on her way to tip a full pan of boiling water down the lavatory bowl.

'*Attention!*' she shrieked. 'Oh, you wicked girl. You

frightened me. *O, là-là, là-là, là-là!* This is boiling water! If I'd spilt it ...! Careful.' Alain and Ella were standing by the door. She eyed her son-in-law with distaste.

'He's ugly,' she had once said to Ella. 'Ugly. Ugly and old. On the wedding day – not a single photograph. Not a single one! And you know why? He'd forbidden it. And she so young,' she'd paused, remembering her daughter only four years before. 'A beautiful young girl. Twenty-one. Innocent.'

She gingerly put the pan down on the floor before opening the door to the closet – the cat went over to the water, then leapt back from the heat – Ella recoiled from the emerging stink. Madame Vinelli sniffed audibly.

'The drains are bad today. The drains,' she tutted, then disappeared with her pan into the hell-hole and they heard the sloshing of water.

'Have you got the bread, Alain?' as she re-emerged, closing the door behind her.

'I'll go down now.' He turned and went back outside.

'A *bâtard*, not a *baguette*,' she cried after him, 'and not too brown.'

Saturday was the day when mother and daughter went into Paris for lunch, followed by the cinema. Madame Vinelli, a smart woman who took great care of herself, worked throughout the week in Paris. She had been widowed a long time and when she'd married, in 1938, a life as a bank employee had hardly been the one she'd expected.

'Ah! Simone!' she called, as the child ran into her bedroom and scrambled up onto her high bed. 'Ella, take charge of her, I want to dress.'

Marguerite Vinelli was French born but, as her name indicates, she had married an Italian, a man from a wealthy banking family. She recounted this to Ella many, many times, and frequently reminded her son-in-law that, though not exactly of aristocratic birth, her marriage into this wealthy Italian family was the next best thing. Aristocrat she might not be, but she certainly was *distinguée* and, needless to say, where her son-in-law was politically on the left, she was most firmly on the right. *La Fauvette* had been built by her husband.

'It used to be quite grand, you know,' she would tell Ella. 'Vegetables, flowers, fruits – and an English lawn. Now look at it! Rack and ruin and weeds. But what can you expect from such an ugly man?'

Sissy started to jump up and down on the bed and there was a loud crash as a framed photograph on the bedside cabinet slipped over.

'*O, mon Dieu!*' shrieked the older woman. 'My husband! My husband!' She rushed over to the photograph, expecting to find the glass shattered. 'Not broken? No, not broken.' Turning it over, she carefully checked the back fastenings. 'But it could have been broken,' and she wagged a finger at the child. 'Ah, my dearest love.' Pressing the frame to her bosom, she sat down on the edge of the bed.

The story of her husband was nothing new to Ella: she'd heard all this before, in fact, everyone who came into contact with Madame Vinelli knew the well-worn tale. At her place of work, they were sick to death of hearing about the wondrous Monsieur Vinelli, his heroism, his patriotism – although not towards France – and, above all, his adoration of his wife.

'Died so young,' she would say, 'a flickering light – extinguished.' (Madame Vinelli was a devotee of romance films, whilst her daughter preferred psychological dramas and the occasional *policier*).

The photograph of her husband was barely visible beneath the lipstick kisses smudged over the glass. 'Now there was a man!' Ella was asked to take it in her hands, to admire the cut of the chin, the Italian hauteur. She found repellant and certainly embarrassing the sluglike imprint of the pursed lips, but she smiled and quickly replaced it on the gilded cabinet.

Madame Marguerite Vinelli, formerly Marguerite Charrier, had married in 1938, but when Italy had declared war on France in 1940, her husband had returned to his homeland to be conscripted into the army – *Capitano*, of course. As she told her tale, Madame Vinelli's sorrow would slide over the desertion of his new wife, for this was how things were, she said, in war there is little choice for many, and of course, she was right. It was only natural that a man should return to his homeland. She never saw him again after that summer of 1940, except for once, and about this meeting, when talking to Ella, she was strangely reticent. However, he had written to her regularly over the next few years. Once, when she was alone with Ella, she had opened the top drawer of that same bedside cabinet, to show a little bundle of letters tied with red ribbon.

'Blood and love,' she had said, and Ella had watched as she had pressed her scarlet lips to the satin bow, and been shocked when she had suddenly hissed – '*Assassiné*.' Adding, with real vengeance: 'the communists, ah yes, Ella, the communists. You're too young to know of these things. Such things – such things – that take place in war.' She had shaken her head in exasperation at Ella's little knowledge of how things had been then – the difficulties, the tragedies – attributing her ignorance to Englishness and island insularity. 'You're too young. How can you appreciate the horrors we endured. He was murdered.' She had grasped Ella's hands, clasping them in her own, as if in prayer, and then had looked upwards to the ceiling.

'God? Monsieur Tessier?' Ella had asked, half joking, not sure whether or not Madame Vinelli could be serious.

'No. Of course not. One doesn't care,' she had glanced at the crucifix over the bed, and as a precaution made the sign of the cross, 'and the other's too ugly to know anything at all about such things.'

On this occasion, perhaps because Sissy was still clambering around on the bed, she did not open the drawer to reveal the letters, nor did she mention murder, but she did beckon to Ella to sit down beside her, so that she could explain how she had never remarried and never could have remarried.

'My heart was broken, you see. Quite broken.' And, as Ella looked at the tears in her eyes, and at the creased skin around the mouth, where the lipstick was seeping down the tracery of cracks in her make-up, she believed in this sorrow and regretted any revulsion and humour which she might have carelessly shown. Tears began to slide down the woman's heavily powdered cheeks, and the girl felt sorry for her. She wasn't to know then what she was later to discover, that this broken heart was indeed irreparable but for rather different reasons from those she had first supposed.

Her daughter, Madeleine Marie Antoinette, had been born in 1943.

III

'There's a man at the bottom of the lane.' It was Monday, still dark, and Madame Vinelli was pottering about in her kitchen on the ground floor, getting ready to leave for work. On weekdays, they all had independent breakfasts, apart from Sissy, who had to sit down, under Ella's supervision, to something substantial. The others took it on the hoof, moving around with a bowl of coffee, dipping in yesterday's bread to soften it and make it more edible. On Sundays they had *croissants*, *brioches* and *pain de mie*. Madeleine was the only one whose 'hooves' were not clattering over the parquet and marble flooring: her breakfast was brought to her in bed and made up of freshly squeezed oranges, white coffee and *biscottes*.

'There's a man there,' Madame Vinelli said, addressing anyone who might be around. Ella went to the back door and looked out. The sky was just beginning to lighten, the air was cold after another night of hard frost. She shivered and closed the door.

'I can't see anyone,' she said as she went back to the bedroom she shared with Sissy. Getting on her bed, she snuggled the eiderdown round herself. Madame Vinelli followed her in, still in her dressing-gown but with full make-up, gold earrings and a chunky necklace.

'He was there last night. I saw him as I came home. A man in a raincoat standing there looking up at the house.'

'Well, he's not there now.'

Sissy began to cry. Ella flung off the eiderdown and went over to her cot, lifting the little child down onto the floor. There was the strong smell of pee. 'Oh, Sissy! Have you done a *pi-pi* in your bed, again?'

The grandmother came over to examine the sheets, wrinkled her nose and sniffed the bedding. 'Tsk! Tsk! Too much liquid before bed-time,' and the man in the raincoat was forgotten as sheets were stripped from the cot and placed for washing by the door into the cellar.

The following day brought two men in raincoats.

'As I came home last night, I could see them – standing right there, just in front of the house,' Madame Vinelli said, as she unbolted the door to set off to work. She pointed to the exact spot. 'Standing there, looking – they were trying to look at us.' She peered out into the gloom to check that they had departed. So bad was her agitation that her daughter insisted that Alain should drive her mother into Paris before going to Nanterre. He agreed, but with great reluctance. It was going to make him late, and he'd been anxious to get to the University early that day, of all days. God only knew what he would find there, since he believed that students had broken into the Dean's office and were even now occupying the administrative block. He'd heard that the University was going to be forced to close and that demonstrations on the Nanterre campus had become increasingly volatile since the arrest of a student who'd taken part in a big anti-Vietnam demo. There were more and more banners, graffiti like coloured spaghetti winding all over the walls, and a growing sense of something that could only be described as physical heat. He could feel it in the air, as soon as he entered the place, his heart started to race. Although a cliché to speak of tingling nerves, his went berserk, like live wires, when he tried to get through to his room.

Ella said again that she had observed nothing unusual outside the house. 'I expect they're just ...,' but her voice trailed away. To herself she thought that they were figments of the older woman's imagination. She'd noticed something like this in Madame Vinelli in the past. The woman did not care for the police, and when two *agents de police* had come to the house from headquarters at Argenteuil to see Ella, Madame Vinelli, who had happened to be home at the time, had been very upset indeed. It was about something and nothing, simply that Ella's residence permit, her *carte de séjour*, needed to be regularized, but Madame Vinelli had gone straight to her room, and Ella had seen that she had left the bedroom door slightly ajar and was peeping through at the policemen in the hallway. When they left, she shot out, agitated, demanding to know what it was that they had come about.

'Were they asking about me? What did they want to know? What did you tell them? Never speak to the police. Never, d'you hear. Never.'

On Saturday, she insisted that she had seen three men, all wearing raincoats and all intent upon studying the house. On the Sunday, she flew into a rage over the man who had come to mend the wire netting round the chicken run.

'What's that *espèce de saleté* doing at the bottom of the garden?' (translated as 'bit of filth') she asked. 'Get rid of him!'

Ella had mentioned all this to Alain, and he had shrugged his shoulders and smiled. 'Don't worry. She's getting old' – forgetting, no doubt, that she was only a few years older than himself – 'A silly old woman. What can she possibly have to hide? She gets stupid like this from time to time. Just placate her – indulge her!'

Things came to a head a week later, when the raincoated figures had multiplied to six: quite a bunch of them, in fact, or so she said. Madame was in and out of her bedroom, peeking through the shutters looking out onto the back lane, and reporting back to the others what was going on. Only Ella took any notice. When she first went outside, she confirmed, as usual, that there was nobody to be seen, but a second time, on her way to the dustbin, she saw, indeed, a group (probably four rather than six) of dark raincoated figures, huddled together at the bottom of the lane. And this time, Alain Tessier had seen them too. No longer seeking to remain undercover, they were now openly observing the house and its occupants.

'Who are they?' Ella asked him. 'What do they want?'

She and Alain were standing downstairs at the back door, still looking at the men, who, in their turn, were staring at them: there was now no furtive lurking, but rather like animals, their eyes engaged, waiting for the other to retreat. It was Alain who was the first to give way. He spread his hand in a gesture of annoyance, his lips set, and closed the door. With a jerk of the head he signalled Ella to follow him upstairs. Madeleine had not yet got up, Sissy was playing in her cot, and Madame Vinelli had retreated to her room.

Alain shut the door of the study and sat down at his desk, turning the chair round to face Ella who was already seated on the divan by the wall.

'Well?' she said again. 'Just who are they?'

'Things are pretty bad in Nanterre. Students are occupying parts of the University and it'll be shut down – that's the way things are going. It's being handled badly.' He paused, twisting the gold signet ring on his right hand.

'What will happen? Why those men – here?'

'Fear. What it comes down to, as so often, it's fear. I don't know what's going to happen, but it's certainly getting way out of control – way out of control. Students are trying to involve the workers – I mean they're involved already – and if they do really come out in the fight – well, who knows where we're gong to end up. It's the speed with which it's all accelerating. Agitators are whipping up support here and across frontiers, and I mean agitators. This is no game. We're not talking about single issues, either, though Vietnam is most often the focal point, but there's so much else falling under that banner.' He ran his fingers through his thinning hair. 'It's old and young – it's certainly over-crowding – too many students and out-dated and inadequate teaching.' He sat down next to her and placed his head in his hands. Ella thought how tired he looked. She sat silent, waiting for him to continue, but for a moment, he said nothing further.

She hesitated. 'Those men?'

He looked up. 'Ah, yes, those.' He bit his lower lip. 'Who are they?'

'We're getting well and truly used to them at the University. The *flics* – police – that's who they are. Little men who think they've got big important roles to play. On the sly before – now – in full view. Watching things, watching us – there they are – standing at the back during meetings, on the edge at demos, sitting in on classes. One of them next to me in the urinal. I peed on his shoe.' He laughed.

'But what are they doing here?'

'On the campus – and elsewhere – they want to identify ringleaders – that's what they say. They're out and about! Taking photographs, taking notes – they stand around with their little notebooks, making their presence felt. Wanting to pin-point agitators,' he smiled. 'But the students have been taking photos of them – pretty pictures of them in their raincoats – pinning them up on the notice-boards surrounded by red graffiti – out with the paint – they're pretty quick to identify the *flics*. They're watching us and we're watching them! What a farce! Undercover agents, standing around in their raincoats with their cameras. What a bloody farce!'

'But what are they doing here, I mean, here, in Montesson?'

He laughed. 'I'm one of the ringleaders – well that's how they'd like to see me! Some ringleader! They got me on camera at the last big anti-Vietnam march, megaphone in my hand. I've had some of them sitting in on lectures. Anything mildly political – anything *they* see as subversive – your name's in the book.'

'But they can't do anything, can they?'

'They know that students come to my room – when I stay overnight. They know that students come here, too. You can see the logic – the way their little minds work.' He went over to the window and looked out. 'It looks as if they've gone. You see, they haven't been able to contain things. I suppose as long as it was in Nanterre – well, anyway, it's well and truly in Paris, now. Reaction at the top's been indecisive. They don't know how to deal with it, and the danger's if they take the hard line, too hard a line – as they're doing.'

'You make me frightened.' She went over to stand by him at the window.

'Be afraid. You're right to be afraid. This is for everyone. Words like 'Revolution' are bandied about. Careless? Well, I don't think it'll take much to shift 'disturbances' and 'unrest' to 'revolt,' 'riot' – 'conflagration' – we're there, or nearly there and it's bloody worrying.'

It was true that groups of students did come to the house and quite frequently, whether or not their professor was there. They went up and down the lane revving up their motor scooters and revving up their excitement. Before now, Ella had seen the local police clearing them away, but she'd never thought anything of it, other than highspirited young – no older than herself: she'd sometimes gone out to chat to them. When Alain was there, he'd been known to invite them in, and they'd gathered together in the study upstairs, sitting on the floor round his desk. Once Ella had counted ten of them squashed into what was quite a small room, and she had squeezed in and stood by the door to listen to what was going on.

Watching Alain hold discussion groups wasn't a new situation for her, since she, herself, had been one of his students at Nanterre, although not officially. In the previous year, 1967, her place had been as a young English girl, nineteen, following a language course, but Alain Tessier was a prominent figure in the University, and his lectures were well attended, even by students from Faculties other than Social Sciences. Curiosity had first encouraged her to go along, when she had first seen the students, as well as a few staff, pushing into his classes, but it was interest which had made her want to continue going.

Although a reserved man, and hardly an extrovert, when teaching he stepped into another's skin. The demarcation between teacher and taught became less sharply drawn, and he identified with and involved the students. Perhaps it was because he had been such a solitary child, but whatever the causes, students liked his style. It made a refreshing change from many other classes attended, where notes were quite literally dusted off each year, reproduced in a tone which advertised that the speaker had long ago loosened engagement with what he (rarely 'she') was saying. Students would look at the pile of lecture notes, the teacher seated behind them, and watch as page after page was read out. Slowly, so slowly, the pile would lower, and there would be a deep sigh as the last page was placed on the completed stack of words. The oft repeated scrawls on the campus walls were not idle comments.

PROFESSORS YOU ARE OLD
Give way to the young

When students left the Tessier lectures, they would often gather in animated groups around the campus. He frequently followed his huge classes with smaller seminars, and on occasions Ella went to these as well. Her French wasn't too good at that time, but she had enough to follow what was going on, and anyway it was just exciting to be amongst them all, listening to raised voices and arguments, watching the verbal, and sometimes physical, pushing and shoving, and discovering when to get out of the way. It all seemed very grown-up and alien. Even then, a year before, she had seen agitators – although she hadn't fully identified them as such, at the time – moving amongst them, deliberately provoking trouble. But it was on one evening, after a meeting in a local café, one where students regularly gathered, that she had first got to talk to Professeur Alain Tessier. The boys, still on the edge of men, strove to take on their masculine roles, often relegating girls to the sidelines of debates, never assuming that they had much to contribute to what were often little more than displays of testosterone-fuelled energy. She was just one more girl tagging onto the tail-end of meetings, new to all this, anxious and exhilarated by turns.

It was a September evening, in 1967. The air was sultry, suggesting rain, and people were sitting outside at the pavement tables as the sun went down, taking the last of the summer weather. The leaves of the trees along the roadside were beginning to fall and the late sun, from time to time, came out from behind the clouds and caught the golden leaves, giving a last burst of fire. There was everywhere, or so it seemed to Ella as she thought back to this time, a regret for the summer's passing.

She remembered so well that night, and saw herself sitting amongst a group of students inside the Nanterre café, not far from the University campus. The inside of the café was darkened, thick with the mingled smells of Gauloises, coffee, wine. Tables had been drawn together and Alain was at the centre. Empty bottles and glasses had not been collected because the waiters couldn't get near, and anyway, they must have sensed the closeness of the group and didn't want to break through. But it was getting late, and one or two students were beginning to drift away, ones and twos, couples with their arms round each other. Ella was on her own, and she had lingered, reluctant to let the evening end and go back to her room alone. Too much wine had been drunk and the conversation was getting silly and more and more argumentative. Bored, she noticed that Alain Tessier had also had enough. The debate was turning into a free for all and one or two of the more vociferous students were beginning to get nasty.

It was difficult to catch all that was being said, particularly when voices were raised and students started to vie with one another, their voices criss-crossing in a babble. Her attention had been caught by a young man and woman at a table outside. The young woman, little older than Ella herself, had turned away from the man, no more than a lad really. Their child, a boy in dungarees – *salopins* – a two-year-old who must have recently found his feet, was given no attention by his parents, and he ran back and forth on the pavement, then took his buggy and pushed it bang up against the wall of the café. With difficulty, he jerked it round and ran back, bumping it against chairs and tables.

[margin note: Not invented in '67]

The young father was speaking to the mother, urgently, but her gaze remained turned away. He touched her arm, and she shook it free. Ella wondered what they were saying. Neither looked at the child. When the woman turned further in her seat, so that her back was towards the man, Ella saw that she was pregnant, and very visibly so. Perhaps they were arguing about that – what to do next? The little boy abandoned the buggy and went to stand against the café wall, picking up small stones and tossing them along the pavement. Now and again, he looked at his parents, occasionally, tentatively, saying – '*Papa*! *Maman*! *Regardez-moi*,' but they didn't turn, engrossed in their own dispute.

After a little while, the child wandered further along the pavement, then began to run in and out of the roadside trees. He bent to pick up a stick and threw it into the road. He stepped off the pavement. A car screeched to a halt.

'Michel!' screamed the mother. The father ran to scoop up the child. Customers in the café stood up. The wife of the patron hurried from behind the bar: '*O mon Dieu!*'

He was alright. He'd only stepped into the gutter, but the driver had thought that he was going to run across. He mopped his brow and waited a few seconds before restarting the engine. The young mother, holding the little boy close to her, smiled towards the other customers, shaking her head. Even from where Ella was, she could see the tears in her eyes. The father put his arm round the mother and his son. He held them tight. They strapped the lad back into the buggy. The mother looked up at the young man and he bent to kiss her.

Ella watched them embrace and her eyes followed them as they set off up the road, arms linked, pushing the buggy together, every now and again turning to each other. It was getting dark.

'I'm going. *Salut!*' Alain abruptly stood up, emptied his glass and was moving towards the door. A few others followed. Ella's attention snapped back to the interior of the bar and she prepared to leave too. The patron came over and there was an argument with a couple of the students over an unpaid bill. Alain turned back and settled it, laying a few notes in the saucer.

'You understand, Monsieur Tessier . . .' The patron was apologetic. He shrugged and held his hands out, palms upturned. Alain, in his turn, raised a hand to signal that nothing further should be said. The patron's wife came over and started to collect the bottles, turning to add something about the young and how she understands but still ...

'Even so, Monsieur, we've got a business to run, you know. We've got the rest of the clientèle.'

'Don't worry,' said Alain, and he dropped a few coins into the saucer. 'I understand. I know. Well ...' and, again, he'd held up his hand to prevent further dispute.

'I mean ...,' said the patron. 'It's like this ...' he shrugged. 'Huh? You know how it is.'

'It's okay. Okay.'

There'd been nervous smiles. The patron placed a hand on Alain's shoulder, and the two men shook hands. Alain had turned to the patron's wife and touched her arm.

'Goodnight Madame. Don't worry about it. It's alright.'

Three or four students went over to the jukebox; another two went to play *Babyfoot*. Ella hooked her bag over her shoulder and followed the rest out into the street, past the pavement drinkers. People were laughing. The patron watched them go and shook his head. He turned to some of the other customers and continued to explain to them the difficulties he faced. His wife went back behind the bar and carried on washing the glasses and coffee cups.

The road was still busy with motorists, as the straggle of students, Alain at the head, turned down a side street, just to the right of the café and leading down to the main thoroughfare. A Lambretta revved its engine behind them, signalling them to get out of the way.

'Okay,' shouted one of the lads, and gestured obscenely towards the rider.

The others laughed, and deliberately slowly they shifted over to the side of the road, closer to the wall on the right, to let the scooter pass, but only just. There was more jeering and fists raised in salute. The tyres skidded on the cobbles, and as it passed Ella, the young rider reached out and caught hold of the strap of the bag slung over her left shoulder, she'd been holding it to prevent it from sliding down her arm.

'Hey!'

She clutched onto it tightly, too tightly, instinctively – she wouldn't let go. All was happening so quickly and she just didn't think. She was still grabbing on – and then she was screaming and he shouting 'Gerroff, you stupid bitch!' and the others yelling at her just to let it go, running after her – trying to get close to pull her off. But she was just keeping on holding the thing. It was her passport, her money – her student identity card, cheque book – but none of this was going through her mind – she wasn't thinking any of this, she was just clinging on for dear life. He was dragging her along with him, until her arm felt as if it was leaving her body. It was crazy of her. Dragged along that cobbled street. She could have been killed. They were all shouting and shouting for her to drop it, but she wouldn't, she couldn't – and then she had to. Her tights were ripped to shreds, and her mini-skirt –

torn to bits if it hadn't been Crimplene, which was virtually indestructible.

The next thing she remembered was that they were all gathering round her and wanting to get her to hospital. They didn't suggest the police, the *flics* were no-go even then. But it was Alain Tessier who cleared them away, called a taxi, and finally agreed that it should be no hospital.

'I'm alright,' she kept on repeating, but of course she wasn't. She looked awful, with a bruised face which she was sure must look like an over-sized turnip. Her legs were badly scratched and grazed: there was blood everywhere. The left shoulder, the one that had had the bag on, was killing her.

'We've got to get you cleaned up,' Alain had said, signaling to the taxi driver to just keep going, wherever. 'You ought to let a doctor look at you. You need to have a check that nothing's broken.'

But Ella had just kept up a quiet weeping, dabbing with his handkerchief alternately at the blood on arms and legs and then at her eyes. Any mention of doctors and hospitals irrationally panicked her. He'd realized that she was in a state of shock and was in two minds about whether to ignore what she wanted and just take her for medical attention, or to take her back with him to Montesson-la-Forêt. The problem with the second option was that it was getting late and Madeleine and her mother would be in bed. There was also the question of his car and whether he could drive with the girl in this state: she didn't seem to know what she wanted and what she was doing. Even under these circumstances he had to admit that he balked at the cost of a taxi all that way.

'Look,' he said. 'Are you listening to me?' she nodded. 'What if I take you to my room at the University? I've got a small bed there and you can sleep on that. You can clean yourself up there and in the morning we'll decide what's best?'

She nodded again, and he had felt that they were

getting somewhere. He directed the cab and took her up in the lift to his room. And then, did she cry! She sobbed and sobbed as if everything inside her was pouring out. She'd wet herself – understandable – and he saw, with some considerable shock what he'd let himself in for. At that time, of course, there didn't seem to be anyone around, although he did hear the sound of voices across one of the quads. It would be students up to God knew what, and he had no intention of getting them involved and worsening the situation.

Somehow or other she managed to get herself reasonably cleaned up in the washrooms at the end of the corridor. He gave her a drink, a brandy, from his stash in the cupboard and got the bed made up. She was asleep almost before he'd said goodnight. He sat up in the armchair in the corner, feet propped on a couple of boxes. In the night he woke shivering. The security light was on in the corridor outside and it cast a dim glow through into his room. He went over to check on her, pulling up the old rug he'd lain across the bed: she was breathing deeply. For a moment he stood looking at her, wondering who she was. Classes were so large that he couldn't have been expected to have noticed her before. Yet, even in the half-light, she looked a pretty girl. He hoped that she'd be fit to leave the next day. Unhooking the old overcoat left hanging on the door, he settled himself back in the chair and wrapped the coat around his shoulders.

When she woke in the morning, for a moment, she didn't know where she was. Looking up, she saw Alain Tessier standing over her, holding a damp handkerchief.

'How d'you feel?' he said, placing the wet cotton over her forehead. 'Stupid question! Pretty dreadful, I should think?'

'I'm sorry,' she said, and he saw her eyes welling up with tears. He felt past it all and didn't want her to start again, but, nevertheless, he gently took hold of her hand, carefully choosing the right one, which was less grazed than the other. 'Listen ... I don't even know your name. Who are you? You're obviously not French?'

She shook her head, eyes filling again.

'Now come on, don't cry. Can you speak French? We've got to sort things out. What nationality? – this is important for the doctors.' He stood up and took a paper and pencil from the desk. 'You've got no identification. I've got to get your name, address, nationality – all the details. Then we'll see about hospital and police.' He waved his hand as she was about to protest. 'Look! Your bag's been pinched. It's an offence. I'll have to know what's in it ... what *was* in it. He'll probably have ditched most of it somewhere. Did you have any money?'

This was how the day went, simply sorting her out, buying her clothes, food, talking to the police, getting her checked over in the hospital. There wasn't a phone at *La Fauvette*, so he rang the butcher and asked him to send the boy up with a message to Madeleine and her mother. Then he remembered that it was Saturday and they'd be in Paris at the cinema and wouldn't get it until they returned. He couldn't leave this girl, and he was uncertain about taking her back home with him and dumping her on Madeleine, who was hardly the best person to deal with the sick and injured – at least not then. It was because he couldn't decide on the best course of action that he took her once again to his room at the University, with a *baguette*, some duck *pâté*, the strongest and foulest smelling cheese he could find, a couple of bottles of wine. If they were going to have to install themselves there for another night, they might as well have some creature comforts. By the early evening, the girl was altogether chirpier and slightly drunk. They started talking about matters other than her wounds; they began laughing. They huddled together in his old greatcoat.

'Have you got a mirror?' She was tenderly touching her face.

'No.'

'A comb – that I can borrow?' Her hair was long, dark

and wavy, and it fell down her back. Yesterday it had been all mussed up, but now he saw that it was thick and caught the light.

'I must look dreadful,' she said. 'D'you think my face'll ever be the same again?'

'It's a lovely face.'

She laughed. 'It's bruised, but it doesn't really hurt now, well, not like it did. What d'you think?' She turned a vulnerable face up towards his, and seemed to want to be loved – or so it seemed to him. She looked weak and lost, like a scared animal, and he knew that he shouldn't take advantage of this fragility, and then that is exactly what he did. She didn't protest as he cupped her chin in his hand and very gently kissed that small anxious face. He kissed her eyes, no longer wet with tears, her bruised cheeks, he licked the small cut across her forehead and then, without at first putting any pressure on her lips, he brushed his mouth against hers and slid his tongue against her teeth, which parted to let him in.

She hadn't meant it to happen. She was young and not at all experienced. Past sexual adventures had been little more than teenage scrambles, unbuttonings and rootings about in darkened places, kids really, discovering each other's secrets – and their own. She didn't know what it could be like and how slow and sweet is that stretched pain, just as she imagined beaten gold thinned and thinned further and further until it breaks into splintering pieces. The bruisings and pains all over her body merged and gathered into a high-pitched hurt of pleasure which only later changed to real physical hurt. Her scratches bled again and streaked and smeared with red the sheet on which they lay.

The following day, Sunday, he took her to *La Fauvette*. They went in the black Citroën, its chassis so close to the road that she seemed to feel every bump along the way. She was a happy wreck. He hadn't mentioned his wife. He hadn't mentioned his child, Sissy. But it was Madeleine who put her to bed, and the bed was in Sissy's room, a large double bed where the cat, Myrtille, slept. It, too, had been found lost and hurt in the forest, amongst the *myrtilles* – the bilberries – and so the two of them were drawn together in sympathy and she was forced to share its fleas. She lay in that bed, with the child's cot on one side of the room, filled with coloured bricks, a play-tray and big board books. The heavy wardrobe stood between them. The shutters were closed, and the little slits of sunlight patterned the parquet floor.

And there she stayed, to become exactly what Madeleine needed, now that her little girl was home – what a stroke of good fortune! Ella, along with other roles, was a welcomed child and husband minder, and her guilt eased when she discovered the dark visits of Charles. The doors opened easily into adultery and Madeleine, with her mannered etiquette, took her by the hand. It was just a way of life.

IV

It was just a way of life.

Once a week, Alain went up to the *source*, the spring at the edge of the forest, which gushed forth its cool fresh water. Those who lived in the area were permitted to take drinking water from this spring, and a hose and a table had been provided, so that people could fill their bottles and small barrels. Residents had a card of entitlement. Ella often went up there with Alain and Sissy, and the child used to like to play around, running in and out of the trees while Ella and her father filled up their bottles, stoppered them and carried the full crate to the boot of the car.

Ella was reminded of the preciousness of water, and thought back to the spring she had visited in the hilly area above Florence, only the previous year: the water, there, bubbling out of the ground, and the small church built around it – a shrine to this source of all life.

There was often plenty of activity around the water point at Montesson-la-Forêt, as people busied themselves with their containers and chatted to other locals about the events of the day over the clink of empty wine bottles. She would watch Sissy, calling to her not to go too far into the woods. It was a meeting place which Ella liked to think was touched with something of the holy, smiling to herself for such fanciful notions. But even so, she imagined, as the water splashed over the bottles, it did seem a timeless place, and this sense of the numinous was helped not a little by the background of swaying coniferous trees, the breeze creating a soft shushing sound, like a breathing within the depths of the forest.

They sometimes went for a walk among the trees; so soon,

they were away from the voices and into the particular darkness found in such a forest, darkness punctuated by pools of light. Different from a deciduous forest, the sameness of the conifers means that there is a sense of walking on and on through an unchanging environment with nothing to mark how far one has journeyed. No particular tree, no unusual twining of roots, like bony fingers, as with oaks and beeches, elms, to tell the traveller that he may have been this way before. The conifers stand tall, like masts of ships, and below lies the soft carpet of pine needles. Ella would look down at this thick bed giving way beneath her feet. The yielding red blanket of fallen needles made her think of blood.

Sissy was not always with them, for if they went up at the weekend, the child frequently chose to stay at home to play with her grandmother, and then they were alone together and could wander through the wood, arm in arm, as if – as Ella imagined they were – a couple in love. Before the cold weather came, in that autumn of 1967, when their fondness for one another was still tentative and curious, wanting to know what it was that attracted each to each, they would lie down on the blanket of fallen needles, deep in the forest, sure that no one would find them, no prying eyes, quiet except for the occasional sound of a gunshot in the distance, which even though far away could still startle her.

'Like a little rabbit,' he said, stroking her face and rolling her over onto her back, pine needles tangled in her hair. 'It's alright, they won't come here. We're still too close to the spring. They're not allowed to hunt this near.'

The trees swung above her in the wind, bending their tops, looking down upon the lovers curled together at their feet. Once a young rabbit came so close that Alain tried to catch it by its ears.

'One for the pot!' he cried.

And she said, 'Oh, no. Not now,' and pulled him back towards her, sliding his hand beneath her sweater and pressing it to her breast. She closed her eyes, sinking deep, deep into the blood-red interior of the earth.

If the weather was bad, the forest would don its fearful face. Its endlessness lost its charm and it became wholly other. No longer beguiling, its darkness turned away from the human, seeming to prohibit entry. And it was on just such a day that Sissy wandered off. Ella had been filling their bottles; there was a queue that morning, perhaps because the weather was bad and it seemed a good opportunity to carry out this chore. It was raining and the water sploshing from the tap had made a muddy pool just where people stood. She had been concentrating upon the bottles – she and Alain were alternating filling and stacking their carriers: she filled while he had stoppered and packed the previous one, then he filled ... and so on – so her attention was taken from Sissy and when she finally looked up, there was no sign of the child.

'Sissy. Sissy,' she called. 'Time to go,' but there was no answer.

'Sissy! Sissy! Where are you?' And her voice was becoming hysterical as she began to prowl the border area between long grass and trees.

'Simone!' shouted Alain, in a sharp voice, concealing his fear beneath affected anger. 'Stop playing. Come along.' But there was still no answering cry.

Ella stepped over the dyke and went into the forest.

'Hey! Ella! Don't you get lost too. We've enough with Sissy.' And she could hear the anxiety in his voice. She waved her hand and continued on into the dark woods. The rain was dripping through the branches and she frequently brushed aside the strands of wet hair hanging down into her eyes. Her shoes were soon sodden from walking on the damp pine needles, now and again kicking fallen cones before her, trying to pretend that any minute she would see the child. She continued to call, stopping every few minutes to listen for any response. The birds were quiet in the rain. She thought that she had gone straight but she hadn't; she had thought that as long as she kept walking in one direction, it would be easy to find her way back, but she hadn't noticed how the slight veering back and forth to avoid trees and mounds over stumps significantly changed her pathway. Very soon, she did not know where she was. She listened for the voices at the source, for the sound of car engines further down the hill, but all was still. Perhaps others were helping with the search, but why couldn't she hear them calling? Why could she no longer hear Alain shouting for his daughter to come back? She shrugged her shoulders and turned, retracing her steps, as she thought, but the longer she walked, the less convinced she became that she was heading back towards her starting-point. She began to talk to herself, to keep her spirits up. The forest was large, and she'd never walked so far into its interior before. She still called out for Sissy and for Alain and was relieved that the rain had lightened and the sky looked a little brighter. She suddenly stopped and leant against a tree, feeling genuinely afraid. How long might she stay in here without being found? But, of course, Alain knew that she was here and a search party would have already been organized for Sissy. She would just remain where she was and wait, calling out from time to time. When she became quite still, she could hear the little sounds of the forest: the plop of rainwater from the trees; the intermittent scufflings from small animals and the occasional birds; noises which were unidentifiable. She thought that she heard the sound of soft regular footsteps – soft, barely determinable – perhaps it was the sound of her own heart, pumping in her ears? Yes, that's what it was. Another regular tread, but this wasn't her ears. For a moment she wondered whether they still had bears in France – wolves? Of course not, and she didn't think that there were wild boars here, but perhaps there were: 'They can have your hand off,' she remembered Monsieur Fontenay's words on the size of these animals and their scissor-action tusks. She held her breath, and closed her eyes, concentrating, to see if she could still hear what seemed to be a steady tread, but the pounding in her ears increased and shut out everything. A hand clasped her arm.

She screamed, or thought she'd screamed, but in reality no sound had come from her mouth, which just hung open in a large round 'O.'

'It's alright! You're alright.'

She hadn't heard him come up behind her, but the ground was so wet and soft.

'Monsieur Gravelin. Ah! *C'est vous!*'

He was standing there in his green hunting gilet, cartridges at his waist, his gun over his shoulder. She began explaining that she hadn't seen him and that she was looking for Sissy and that she'd got lost and was waiting for someone to find her.

'I know. It's alright,' he said again, laughing loudly.' We've found the little Simone. Naughty girl! She was just playing at the edge of the forest. She hadn't gone far at all – just didn't answer. You should have waited and she would have come back. Her Papa's got her and taken her home and I said I'd give you a lift back. I've been following your tracks. Zig-zag – going back on yourself, then round in a big arc. Once lost, it would've been easier if you'd stayed put!'

Monsieur Philippe Gravelin was a family friend and particularly a friend of Alain Tessier, for he worked in the administrative section of the Sorbonne University in Paris, which meant that the two men had much in common. With Charles Fontenay, he and Alain would go hunting. People said that this Monsieur Gravelin lived in the forest, which wasn't, of course, true, though he did have a house right on the edge of that large forested area and he knew it with the intimacy of an animal. In fact, Charles was fond of saying that Philippe Gravelin smelt his way around, tracking prey like a dog, a great big dog, for he was every bit as tall as Charles but looked even bigger, well-padded with muscle and flesh. He wasn't the sort of man anyone would want to tangle with. Alain was dwarfed beside him. Madame Vinelli considered him uncultured and coarse in his behaviour, but then her definition of a man '*comme il faut*' was somewhat limited.

He was a man who got things done. Size and an overbearing manner meant that he bullied others into submission. Living close to the earth gave him a certain brutishness: he knew what he wanted and got what he wanted. It would be fair to say that he was not a man over-endowed with sensitivity. There was certainly nothing squeamish about him, as Ella could testify, having once watched him killing and skinning Sissy's pet rabbit, after his own dog had got hold of it and shaken it to death. In no time at all he had been pulling off the soft fur coat like a suit of clothing from a manikin, peeling it back like a leather glove, and she had rushed the wide-eyed Sissy indoors. Ella was wary of him, wary of the thick accent which she could not always understand, wary of the pungent smell of the man, wary of a seeming unpredictability in his behaviour.

'It's alright – alright! You've nothing to fear, little English girl,' and he squeezed her arm. She looked down at the spade-shaped hand still gripping her as he propelled her back towards the spring. The hand pressed against her breast and, for the first time, she thought about the probability of his having been in the forest when she and Alain were alone together. As she knew him to be a man who spent his life prowling the woods, this was no idle speculation. She looked up at him, and he smiled, again the fingers squeezed her arm with a disturbing familiarity.

'Don't you worry, little English girl.'

That evening Philippe Gravelin stayed for dinner. When the soup tureen was passed to him, he fished around with the ladle for bits of chicken and pulled up the foot and claws of the bird.

'Ah!' Madame Vinelli looked at her daughter, who was eating nothing. 'Why didn't you strain the soup?' and there followed a fractious debate about preferences for soup which had passed through the mouli-sieve, pulping the vegetables as opposed to leaving them in large pieces: Madame Vinelli liked the former but her daughter and Philippe favoured the latter, both saying that they wanted to be able to recognize the different vegetables and meats and weren't into eating pap like a baby.

'Act as judge and jury on this, Alain,' said Madeleine, but he didn't answer, he didn't even seem to hear, staring down at his soup dish in a preoccupied way. Ella wondered whether he had been listening to anything said throughout the entire evening. His wife shook her head, and after this there was no further conversation. Philippe Gravelin noisily slurped his soup and ripped off chunks of bread with his fat fingers, dunking them into the hot liquid. There was an undeniable tension in the room, even Sissy recognized it and fell silent, eventually falling asleep in her highchair.

'*Ma cocotte*,' cried her grandmother. 'Look at the little thing, Madeleine! Ella, it's time for her *dodo*.' Before Ella could lift the little girl down and carry her off to bed, Madeleine stood up, pushed back her chair and left the room.

'And for us,' said Alain, abruptly, 'it's time to be off. It's eight-thirty and we've got to be in Paris in an hour's time.' He glanced at his watch, then at Philippe Gravelin, but ignored his mother-in-law.

Philippe stood up and placed an arm round his friend's shoulder.

'Good luck, my friend. *Bonne chance*,' and turning towards Madame Vinelli, 'I'll see myself out. Thank you.'

Madeleine appeared from the bedroom, wearing a light coat and carrying a small leather suitcase.

'Goodbye, Ella, I shall be back in a couple of days. Maman will tell you what needs doing.' And with that, all three left the house.

A little later, after having got the child to bed, Ella was washing the dishes in the upstairs kitchen (apart from Sunday and special days, the family ate upstairs), when Madame Vinelli joined her, agitated and tearful.
'She's gone for an abortion.' It was straight in, no preliminaries.
'Ah!'
'His fault.' Her look spoke volumes. Ella immediately thought of Charles Fontenay. As if in answer to those thoughts, Madame Vinelli looked meaningfully towards the bedroom. The door of the Tessier bedroom was shut, but Madame Vinelli tapped across the marble floor in her high heels and turned the handle. Ella followed and peered cautiously in. The shutters were half-closed and it took a moment for her eyes to adjust. She saw the voile curtains shifting slightly in the evening breeze, on the bed clothes were strewn about, more were tossed across the chairs either side of the window. Drawers were not quite shut, and she could see into the long one beneath the chest. It was full of Madeleine's shoes, strappy stilettos. Her clothes, his clothes lay twisted together on the bed. Ella turned away and went back to the kitchen. She hadn't wanted to see this, just as she hadn't wanted to acknowledge anything other than her own love for this man. Of course he loved her, she thought, and of course she knew that she didn't want to think otherwise.
'Conflagration' and 'revolution' were words alien to her vocabulary, and in a similar way 'adultery' and 'betrayal' were used by and about others but did not apply to herself. When Madame Vinelli had gone to bed, Ella went back into that bedroom, turning on the bright central light, so that everything appeared sharply distinct, like a theatrical set. She stared round the room as if it had nothing to do with her: in reality it had everything to do with her. There was a broken water glass on the floor, recently spilt, and the water had seeped into the polished parquet, leaving a dark stain. She bent down and picked up a piece of glass, ran her fingers over that damp brown

stain. A nightdress lay crumpled beside it, where it had presumably been tossed earlier in the day, and she gathered it up, as if to place it on the bed, then let it fall – together with the jagged glass – back onto the floor. As she did so, she saw that two small square envelopes had also been carelessly dropped and she instinctively bent down to pick one of them up.

'*Glissez le membre ...,*' she read. But this wasn't Charles. She knew, she just knew. And she felt that, after all, however much the marriage was dead, she was perhaps no more than a now and again interlude. She had never admitted this to herself and hadn't even allowed herself to consider it. She continued to hold the condom wrapper, knowing, as sure as if he'd told her, that it had nothing to do with Charles Fontenay. She felt an intense jealousy. Dropping the wrapper, she wiped her hands down her skirt. It fluttered to rest upon the shattered glass.

It was later that night, as she lay in bed, the large double bed with its polished wooden headboard – and its fleas – that she thought of the secret, illegal operation which must at that moment have been taking place behind shut doors. To her, the aborted foetus seemed like a symbol for all the incomplete and unfulfilled relationships: a marriage in its death throes; an adulterous affair between Madeleine and Charles, oddly secretive and yet carried out in full view of locals; and her own love, which was for her romantic but, for Alain, perhaps habitual and readily accommodated into the diurnal round. She felt depressed and sullied by it all, tangled, as she was, in this strange mixture of the erotic, the casual, and now the criminal. Although nobody attended mass, Catholic faith was given a nod, certainly by Madame Vinelli, the crucifix positioned above her bed and the Madonna in the hall, who stared meekly down over her bruised chin. Divorce was out of the question. If Charles had fathered this child, it was Alain who was with Madeleine now, and Ella wondered where Philippe Gravelin fitted into all this.

That night, in the bathroom, she had looked down at her stomach, looked at it this way and that in the mirror, searching for any signs of visible rounding and, on and on, throughout the night, she continued to think about what was happening somewhere in Paris, imagining it all as a dark and sordid act, a criminal act, where discovery had terrible consequences. She felt it as her own taint, her guilt. She wanted to get away from this place and leave it all behind her, and she cried for the lost child as if it were her own.

The next week, Alain was sitting in the bare salon upstairs, cleaning the hunting gun he kept in the big cupboard, when she told him that everything must end. Madame Vinelli and Madeleine had gone to Paris for their Saturday visit to the cinema. Sissy was playing in the corner, and the child looked up from time to time, as if sensing the strain in the room. He took gun cartridges out of the drawer in the desk and arranged them in a row, slowly, one by one, the heavy gold signet ring on his right hand tapping against the edge of the desk. Sissy came over to him, attracted to them as playthings.

'Papa?' She held out her hand.

'No, Sissy, definitely no!' and then to Ella, 'but why? Why?' He spread his hands to show his incomprehension.

'Madame Tessier. You didn't tell me you had a wife when I first came.'

'You soon knew. I ask you – why?'

'I can't.'

'But, why? Did you mind before? You gave no sign of it. If you think she minds, you're wrong.' Ella started to say something but he silenced her with a wave of his hand. 'Of course she knows. She's always known. She has her own ...,' he stopped, as if searching for the right word, 'satisfaction.'

'Last week. It could have been me' – and under her breath, 'the baby.'

'Don't be silly. I'm careful – well, you know that. Don't let's be stupid about this. You know that you can trust me,' his voice softened, and he sat silent for a minute or two. Ella watched Sissy playing, and now and again, Sissy looked up at her. She was the sort of child who knew when not to interrupt the grown-up world.

'You have meant so much to me, Ella,' he finally said, and shrugged his shoulders. She wanted to believe him.

'Shall I leave – I mean leave for good?' and as she said this, she was aware that she was pleading with him to say no.

'Of course not. Things work well. These problems will pass.'

'No, I don't think so,' she didn't want it to be included in 'problems,' as if all that she had felt were no more than an inconvenience. 'I really don't think so. You've been teaching me to grow up and I'm growing up.'

'Where will you go? Back to England?'

'Not yet, not just yet.'

He picked up the cartridges and tossed them from hand to hand, and they clicked against his ring. When he pushed back his chair, the gun toppled over onto the parquet, making them all jump. 'Give it a rest – for a while. Think about it. Nobody's been hurt. We've been happy. We have been happy, haven't we?' and he laughed. 'Is it the English puritanism, is that it? Yes, think about it, *mon petit chat.*' And then with that gentleness she'd always found so appealing – 'life's short. Ella, listen to me. I'm very fond of you, my little one.' Sissy thought that he was talking to her, and she got up and put her head on her papa's knee. He ruffled her hair affectionately. 'Ah, yes, the two of you. I wouldn't hurt either of you. No, really. When you're happy, take what life has to offer,' and again, he said, 'we're hurting nobody and as for ... you can trust me to look after – all that. I was once a good Catholic, and I know how to manage things. I can square it with my conscience.'

There was a knock at the outside door and a voice calling. Sissy went back to her playthings and began to pile her mother's *bigoudis* into Ella's lap, and the girl looked down at the coloured hair rollers and the plastic sticks used to hold them in place, and smiled at the intrusion of such ordinariness, and all that they seemed to represent. Alain grinned.

'See, *ma puce*. That's what life is. Let's take happiness where we can. Don't fret, you know. I'll take care of you. I'll always take care of you.' They heard the outside door open and heavy footsteps on the stone staircase.

Philippe Gravelin was accustomed to walking straight in on a Saturday afternoon, when the other two women were usually out. He flung open the door of the study, his bulk filling the doorway, and he looked straight at Ella and Alain, the two of them seated so close together, and little Sissy between. His eyes went from one to the other, but he said nothing. Then he gave one of his huge raucous laughs. Alain stood up, picking up the gun and cartridges. The two men were off hunting.

Ella watched them leave. She looked out of the upstairs window, the one next to the bathroom, and her eyes followed them as they strode down the lane, the larger man ahead of Alain. She'd sometimes seen them on their return from one of these expeditions: Gravelin, with all the little birds round his waist, their heads dangling like tassels. She turned slowly back to find Sissy, recalling a time in November of the previous year. It had been late November when it was growing cold and her breath had hung in the air, and now she remembered watching Philippe Gravelin in the Tessier garden, next to the cellar door where Charles made his habitual entrances. Steps led down to that little area protected from the wind, and he had been sitting on an upturned barrel, a goose across his knees, rapidly plucking it while the flesh was still warm. Just before, she'd seen him wring its neck. The white feathers fell at his feet, like a light covering of snow. The neck hung down between his legs, blood dripping from its beak, scarlet drops upon freshly fallen snow.

He had roared with laughter when he had seen her there, that great belly laugh she would later grow to detest, and he had held out the head of the bird, waving it on its limp neck, like a ball at the end of a rope.

'Come! Come! My little English girl.' He had stretched out his bloody hands and taken hold of one of hers, and the blood had been wet and sticky. She remembered that goose, and she remembered afterwards – when his goose was cooked.

He had come to Sunday dinner especially to eat the goose. He had taken his place at the head of the table in Madame Vinelli's dining-room and had set to, with gusto, to carve the bird, roaring with laughter, giving Madeleine and Ella little morsels to taste, while he picked off bits for himself with fingers greased with fat.

'Madame,' he said to Madame Vinelli, 'a little breast, perhaps?' and while she inclined her head towards him, Ella could see that as he said this he was looking at Madeleine and the slight hint of cleavage which her blouse exposed, her skin still tanned from the summer sun. Little trickles of goose fat ran from the corners of his lips.

On such Sundays, Madeleine brought down her *disques,* vinyl long-players. On this occasion, Edith Piaf was requested, and everyone regretted that she had died some years before and reflected on the endless gossip surrounding her and her hairdresser lover. Madeleine, Alain and Madame Vinelli had seen her final performance at the famous Olympia theatre in Paris.

'The spotlight on an empty stage,' reminisced Alain, and they all stopped eating for a moment. 'Then she came on. That tiny, tiny figure. Remember?' and all but Ella nodded. 'Looking like a little sparrow, skin and bone, no more – so ill. And the light fell on her and all around was darkness, and she stood there entirely alone and the band began to play – and – my God!' (Madame Vinelli winced) 'the sound of that voice. The power! Could she sing! The sound that came from that sparrow!'

'*Merde*!' shouted Philippe Gravelin, breaking the spell. He'd been carving the second leg and the knife had sliced through his left forefinger. The blood dripped onto the hot goose, and Ella thought that the bird had got its own back. She found it hard to swallow the lump of flesh in her mouth as Philippe sucked at the blood. Madame Vinelli went for a bandage and Alain turned on the record player. At the end of the meal, Philippe sat down too heavily on one of the Louis Quinze chairs and split the webbing.

V

'It wasn't my child,' he had said, and Ella pondered over this. Did he know about the night visitor? Surely he did, but she had to be careful. Could he know that his friend made such regular dark excursions from the cellar? And if he did, how was it that the two of them continued their friendship? Could there be somebody else, perhaps? Each Thursday afternoon Madeleine left for Paris – to attend her Italian class, she said – she always caught the train at a quarter to two, and she always carried nothing other than the smallest of Italian dictionaries.

'*Au revoir*, Ella. See you this evening.'

Ella had grown used to this weekly class, if class it was, for to be honest, she was beginning to wonder about its regularity and most particularly about the size of the dictionary. It did seem a very little covering for another adulterous affair: Madeleine naked upon some bed, the tiny dictionary opened – 'Ah! *Bellissima*!' – a fig-leaf. Curled hair peaking out between the paper leaves.

How could Alain be so sure that the child was not his? Although Ella's anxieties had been temporarily ended by Alain's reassurance, the image of the Tessier bed, the twisted night things, scattered underwear, condom wrappers, remained in her head. How, indeed, could he be so sure that the child was not his?

Italian lessons: grammar or love? Either way, it might be that Madeleine was searching after her lost father. If a lover, Ella imagined him as the dark, proud man in Madame Vinelli's photograph. And so, without further ado, one Thursday afternoon, when Sissy was having her afternoon nap and Madeleine was away with her Italian, when all the house was quiet, curiosity got the better of her. Ella softly turned the handle of Madame Vinelli's bedroom door and went into the darkened room. A little light showed through the closed shutters, just enough for her to see her way around, for she dared not switch on the light, even though she was quite alone.

The bed was neatly made. There was a strong smell of Roget-Gallet *Eau de Cologne*. The heavy furniture lent the room an unpleasantly enclosed feeling, so that, in spite of her reluctance to put on the light, Ella opened one of the windows, just a little, and then, with a loud click, pushed up the retaining lever of the folding metal shutters, and they caught the wind and swung back, rattling against the stone frame. The draught slammed the door shut – she held her breath. There was no one to hear. Sissy slept on. She stood at the bedside, turned the crucifix to the wall, and picked up the photograph of Signor Vinelli.

Madeleine had been born in 1943. Her father had left France to join the Italian army in June 1940. Madame Vinelli had said that she had not seen her husband again, except just once, and that, Ella imagined, must have been when Madeleine was conceived. The family had a house in the south of France, close to the Italian border, and Madame Vinelli had told Ella that it had suffered during the war. In a moment of intimacy, this older woman had confided to her that she, a young woman, alone and unprotected, had travelled to Menton to meet her husband, and Ella had thrilled to hear of this romantic adventure: the one meeting; the conception; the assassination of the husband; the birth of Madeleine! Now this was the height of romance, and she had leant upon the older woman's every word.

Although, at any other time, Madame Vinelli had seemed reluctant to speak of this final time of love, one evening, when all were seated round the dinner table, some casual remark prompted her to launch into a retelling of her story, almost as if she felt obliged to do so. Ella listened, as the bare outlines already given to her were filled out.

It seemed that aged twenty-five, and entirely alone, she had set off in the November of 1942 to meet her husband. The journey had been hard and had taken a number of days, but they had met in secret at the house in the south. In his uniform, he had been waiting for her – so she said – and they had passed there two nights of love.

'*Mon Luigi. Mon amour.*' And she had gone on to tell of an autumn idyll, as if a scene from an Italian opera. Embarrassed, all those round the table stared down at their plates. 'I was his little Marguerite and he gave me my child, my Madeleine. A gift before he died.' She paused before whispering the word '*assassiné.*' Tears trickled down her cheeks and she dabbed at them with a little lace handkerchief, before leaving the room, too distressed by the memories of this ideal love.

For what seemed a very long time, no one had said anything. Sissy had looked from one to the other, after having been cautioned by her grandmother to remain silent while she told her tale. Ella felt extremely awkward as an outsider intruding into such a very private situation. She pushed her chair back, intending to leave the table.

'Don't go!' Madeleine leant over and placed a restraining hand upon her arm. 'Although Maman may seem shy about this, in fact, we've heard it before. Now and again she has to go over it. It's best just to listen, then let it rest.'

Ella resumed her place. 'But is it true? All that she says?'

'No, I think not,' Alain reached out for a piece of bread. 'We hear it, she pretends that she doesn't want to talk about it, but she always does. We, in our turn, pretend that it's new to us. Each time it's an exclusive, for our ears only. Each time, the last time it'll be told before she remains silent forever – until the next time!' He broke a piece of bread and cut a slice of cheese. 'This is for your benefit. She likes the limelight. Over again, the same old story of their meeting before death steps in with his knife, with his gun, who knows how it was? The assassin.'

'Alain!' Madeleine struck her fist on the table.

'I'm sorry,' he cut himself another lump of cheese. 'Your father. I meant no disrespect.'

But later, when he and Ella found themselves alone, he elaborated on all that had been said. 'Of course it's a lie – not quite all, but there's still a plentiful supply of lies. Her bit of play-acting. Didn't you see how she averted her gaze?'

'But she was embarrassed.' Ella brushed aside his criticism. 'How could she not be timid – recounting her own life.'

'Well, well! Pure fantasy – most of it. At that time – France overrun by Germans – do you expect me to believe that a young woman should have set off on such an arduous journey – at such a time? Travelled down through France, all alone, where there were German and Italian troops everywhere – all alone – continued on to the Italian border? I don't think so. I do not think so.'

And now, as Ella stands in Madame Vinelli's bedroom, the photograph of Captain Vinelli in her hands, she remembers the time when Sissy bounced upon the bed and the photograph frame slammed face down onto the cabinet. She remembers, too, the woman's anxiety and sees again how she looked first at the feeble closures on the back, pressing down the small tin fastenings, where now only two remain, the other four having been bent back so many times, again and again and again – and crack, another little folding of tin is broken and falls to the floor as Ella slides her thumb nail beneath and removes the backing to see what lies hidden under Captain Luigi Vinelli's handsome stare.

A piece of faded paper: then an old photograph, much smaller than the one in the front of the frame. It slides out easily, for the edges are rough, like nibbled fingernails, from having been removed so many times.

She turns over the photograph and sees a fair-haired young man of true Aryan blood, light eyes and smiling mouth, and written in faded ink across his chest:

'*Marguerite - mein Schatz. Wolfgang.*'

Dare she look at the letters? She dare. She pulls open

the little drawer and picks out the small bundle of envelopes and sees that the writing is the same as that on the photograph. She cannot bring herself to remove the ribbon. The stamps are not Italian.

She placed the letters, unexamined, back into the drawer. She returned the photograph of Wolfgang, noting the finger prints along the glossy edges. There was now only a single tin fastening to bend back to hold all in place. She searched the floor for the broken fragment but couldn't find it. After closing the shutters and window, she looked round the room to make sure that nothing appeared disturbed. She ran her hand over the counterpane, smoothing away tell-tale wrinkles from where she had been sitting. One last look before closing the door – Ah! – the crucifix turned to the wall!

Instead of relating all this to Alain, she hugged her guilty secret to herself, as if it were her very own little love, her romance, illicit – illegal – concealed behind an exterior absolutely *'comme il faut,'* all as it should be, but for the fragility of the little tin clasps which hid it away, each clasp snapping free from being opened again and again, so that now only one held the secret in place. At night, she snuggled down with this love story and it fed into her dreams, and Wolfgang caressed her while a young Madame Vinelli, Marguerite, looked on, impotent, powerless to reclaim her story.

The time never seemed exactly right to tell Alain of her discovery, or, more accurately, of her theft, for theft it was, and she was well aware that she had entered the room uninvited and had more than pried into another woman's life. It was as if she had taken a knife to this other's heart, easing it open with the pointed blade, folded back the delicate tin clasps, and seen something that she should not have seen, something she had no business to see. She had stolen a secret and made it her own, and as the story of this other love took shape inside her own imagination, it was as if it became her story, her life, and she began to love it as her own.

Wound round with this romance, she barely noticed the turmoil going on around her. Alain slept night after night at Nanterre, drawn into the increasing tensions of student unrest. The streets there sounded with the marching feet, the chants of young and angry voices, but Ella was hardly aware of them, although each time Alain returned, tales of agitation flooded the household. Students continued to visit *La Fauvette* from time to time, and Alain talked earnestly to them in the study. The smell of Gauloise cigarettes and strong coffee defeated the acrid odours from Madame Vinelli's *cabinet*. Meals were served late, if at all.

'Have you bought anything for dinner?' Madeleine asked her mother.

'I thought you were seeing to that tonight?'

'*Tant pis!* Too bad. We'll not eat tonight. A sacrifice to the cause!' Each sat moodily over a glass of wine and a fried egg.

It was when the police, for it was presumed to be the police, forced open the Fontenay mail-box, one Wednesday morning, and then, on the following Saturday, the Tessiers', that Ella raised her head from her dreams. The first act of vandalism could have been some joke or intended violation committed by anyone, they supposed, for the Fontenay name was well known, but the fact that the second took place on the following Saturday, immediately after Charles had deposited his letter and even before the postman had gone by, suggested that this was deliberate espionage.

Ella listened to the raised voices of the two men. She saw Charles's warning nod to Madeleine, who knew for sure that her invitations must find another route. It was an abomination, they said, that there should be such an invasion of privacy. And who knew where it was all going to end, Madame Vinelli muttered, as she tapped her way across the tiles. They'd be entering the house next, searching amongst personal possessions. Was it her imagination or did Ella see a flicker of suspicion that such an entry might already have taken place? Perhaps she had noted that another tin fastening had cracked away? The older woman tutted her way to Paris, increasingly anxious at the rumour that disturbances could spread and threaten her own safety.

Meanwhile, Alain and Charles spoke of using Philippe Gravelin as a go-between, or more accurately a *poste restante*. The letters between the two men had, understandably, quite a lot to say about the events at Nanterre, and it wasn't too difficult to realize that their positions could become uncomfortable, at the very least. Alain was not alone amongst the University staff in supporting the students in many of their complaints, but his name had become worryingly prominent and he had found that some of his colleagues, those he had thought of as friends, even though politically on opposite sides, had started to avoid his company. Charles and Alain decided between them that they should leave their letters with Philippe – perhaps giving them to him at the *source*, for example. This would mean a delay which couldn't be avoided, and even they had to admit that it gave their activities an appealing irregularity. Visits to the spring would become more frequent, more subject to cautious peering around, more a question of subterfuge – a little *résistance* of their own!

If Ella had understood more of the relationship between Alain and Charles, and about how it had formed when they were both students, living together in the same digs, she might have been less surprised at their continuing closeness. Charles, leather-jacketed, always attractive to women, had presented something of a role model for Alain, who'd got into the habit of taking over the other's cast-off girlfriends, rather like putting on a second-hand coat, with the smell and feel of its original occupant still there. Of course, it could work the other way, as was the case with Madeleine, where the route to Charles came via his adjutant, Alain. The two men were always together and the glamour of Charles, Gauloise in the corner of his mouth, thick dark hair, leather jacket slung across the shoulders, was infinitely attractive to women – and to Alain. The thoughtful, scholarly nature of Alain appealed to Charles and taught him to reflect more seriously upon life, in a way which did not come naturally to him. But it hadn't taken Charles long to disengage himself from too onerous an academic course, and instead of going with the grain and following the straight route from examination to examination, he cut across, letting this special time of life feed his creativity. With Alain's last-minute help, he passed his exams – just – and had had two novels published by the time he graduated.

Charles's relationship with women might also be called a cross-grain affair. He enjoyed their company but never allowed any to become permanent attachments. From time to time he would disappear for a while. Alain didn't ask where he had been, nor with whom, and their literary correspondence perhaps reflected this wider free and easy relationship. Although neither of them ever articulated anything about limits, each knew that there was a barrier between them which should never be ruptured and that the stability of their close friendship depended upon that barrier's being maintained.

The house at Montesson-la-Forêt had been in the Fontenay family for many generations. Like Alain, Charles was an only child and although indulged by father and mother, it had been his mother who had taken pride of place in his life, and particularly so after his father's death. He had known Madeleine as a child, he had been nineteen when she'd been born, thirty-seven when she'd completed school and gone to university, so it was understandable that he'd always thought of her as a child. When Alain had first invited him to meet his new '*amour*,' he'd been astonished to find that it was his little Madeleine, the girl from his neighbourhood: how convenient! The arrangement between the three friends became the most easy thing to manage.

VI

Madeleine grew fed up. She was tired with Alain, night after night, staying over in Nanterre to deal with more than disgruntled students. Teaching had been suspended, for a period, and there was a continual stream of complaints around the University: a swell of dissatisfaction. When a number of students were threatened with expulsion and rumours began to circulate that a black list had been drawn up, with certain of them destined for unmerited failure in the forthcoming exams, more and more began taking to the streets.

Down with the Black List

Alain felt increasingly convinced that a similar list was being drawn up for teaching staff and he had an unpleasant feeling that his name could well be at its head; at the very least, his chances of promotion could come to look distressingly unlikely. The whole business was getting nasty, with unpleasant smells from the past, like Madame Vinelli's drains, starting to waft their way down academic corridors. Although the big political disturbances had prominence, as they should, petty and often personal problems were given an airing, like little farts in a corner. Dislikes which had lain dormant, alongside hurts or indignities nursed over long periods, began to reappear: wounds bled afresh.

Charles had gone away on one of his little expeditions, God knew where, certainly Madeleine didn't, for she had had no response to the invitations deposited at the Gravelin house. Night-time visits had temporarily ceased, and although this had happened in the past, it was particularly aggravating for Madeleine when she had little else to occupy her. Italian classes had also stopped for the Easter recess, if classes they were, and her visits to Paris on a Saturday had similarly been suspended because her mother disliked the increasingly threatening atmosphere, as she called it, around the student left-bank area. This was where she and her daughter usually went to see a film, turning up their noses at the price and the sub-titled American films generally showing in the bigger, more fashionable cinemas. Madeleine was reluctant to go by herself: 'A woman alone in the cinema is pestered all the time,' she said. 'My mother keeps them at bay!'

And that was true, as Ella well knew, from her own hopping from seat to seat when she went to a film on her own. She had had plenty of experience of the light fingers at the back of her neck, around her waist, upon her knee – and higher – the brushing against her leg and the hand suddenly clutching her own.

'*Assez*! Enough, will you! Eh, then!'

'Ssssh! Ssssh!' – from various parts of the darkened auditorium. Yes, she understood why Madeleine preferred the protection of her mother.

When Alain did come home, he was tired and not much company. Madeleine sat down to pen yet another letter to Charles.

'*My darling, I miss you,*' she wrote, and then laid into Alain, getting it all onto paper and well off her ample chest. '*He's never here. I miss you, my love. Maman was right. He's just worn out, no good, life's so tedious.*' There then followed a good bit of 'if only.' If only she hadn't married him; if only she hadn't fallen pregnant; if only her husband would simply disappear; if only she and Charles could be together – always and always.

Her pen lingered over the word 'disappear,' and she thought of hunting, and moving in with Charles, and then their removal to Paris. As sometimes happens, her thoughts wiggled their own way down onto the page and added themselves to all the earlier 'if onlys.'

'Ella would you pop up to Monsieur Gravelin's and

put this in his mailbox?' She sealed down the letter to Charles, placing it in a large envelope. Shaking her fountain pen, to encourage the ink to flow more freely, she carefully addressed it to Monsieur Charles J. Fontenay.

It was still raining when Ella set off in the direction of the forest, Sissy trotting beside her in wellie boots and red plastic mackintosh. It had been pouring earlier in the day, and she'd put the letter in her bedroom, waiting for the downpour to lessen. Easter was ten days away, and she'd a strong desire to leave for England. She and Alain still met from time to time, but opportunities had been scarce. Now that Madeleine's visits to the cinema on Saturdays had temporarily been abandoned, any lovemaking while Sissy had her nap had also been curtailed. As they walked up the hill, Ella gave a long sigh, and Sissy stared up at her.

'I love you, Ella,' she said, seeming to sense the young woman's weariness.

Ella squeezed her hand. 'And I love you, Sissy.' But did she also love him – Alain? At the start, she had certainly felt a passionate interest in the man, but perhaps the charm had come in part from the furtive meetings. There was no doubt that gentle squeezings, secret kissings, touchings behind the kitchen door or passings on the stairs, as well as brief meetings behind the wall beyond the apple trees, close to the chicken run, had given a certain piquancy to their romance. And then, of course, there were the delights of the forest on a Sunday, after the market, Sissy safely left with her grandmother. Even the cold and damp, the driving into the woods, away from habitation, and into that special gloom, presented wicked pleasures. They had a rug and Alain's old overcoat, the very one beneath which they had first snuggled down in his room at Nanterre. The secret burrowing together beneath the folds of thick, smelly tweed, despite, or because of cold and rain, was a delicious, if not too delicate, adventure.

Sometimes the drops of rain would fall down from the branches – from so high, like blessings from heaven – down upon their upturned faces. The obligatory cigarettes, trying to keep the match alight and giggling like a couple of kids. And always, the slow swaying of the trees and the smell of pine needles, of damp wool and musty wood. Well, thought Ella, squeezing Sissy's little fingers between her own, if it wasn't love, it came damned close!

Sissy ran over to a puddle. Ella waited while the child splodged about. She smiled towards the daughter of Alain and Madeleine and wondered again whether she loved him and the extent to which love is bound to the hope of fulfilment – of ever after. Perhaps she, like Madeleine, would grow weary of snatches of pleasure and want the certainty of knowing that she was always in his mind, there to come home to, each for each, night after night. Love, she thought, is a selfish thing. It can't seem to manage with small helpings, now and again, it wants a plateful – anyway, she, for sure, wanted the full menu, but perhaps for him, and for Charles as well, the now and again and the absence of total commitment really was enough.

'Don't do that, Sissy! Look! It's all going in your wellies.'

No question of divorce, he would never leave Madeleine. Maybe, for men rather than for women, she wondered, it is easier to be loyal to two? She patted the letter tucked beneath her coat. Perhaps for Alain it was the impermanence and the risk which partly satisfied, as, for a while, it had done for her. Ella kicked a pebble into the next puddle: but now she found that the danger was beginning to pall. In place of excitement, she was discovering anxiety; in place of longing was a recurring sorrow at parting. Like Madeleine, she was beginning to feel increasingly lonely.

The rain had started again, in earnest.

'Hurry! Sissy, come on.'

They reached Gravelin's house, and Ella lifted up the child, so that she could put the envelope in the box.

'Be a postman, Sissy. *Hop-là!* In it goes.' And in it didn't. The envelope was too big and it fell down into the mud. Ella picked it up and wiped it with her sleeve, but the mud and the wet stuck to the face of the envelope and smudged the name and address. She folded it over and stuffed it into the box, as best she could. An edge still stubbornly stuck out.

The following Saturday, all the family went to visit a relative living south of Paris. Ella was invited to join them but declined, saying that she would like to profit from a free day by going into the city, where there was an exhibition at the Grand Palais that she particularly wanted to see. In the event, when she got there, the queues were enormous, and after having waited for over an hour and barely moved forwards, she decided to scrap it and go for a walk in the Tuileries gardens, and then on to the Champs-Elysées. It was a lovely spring day, and she sat by the boating pond, feet up on a green metal chair, face turned to the sun. Children were running round the pool, pushing with long sticks their blue yachts, most of them on loan from the nearby kiosk. The breeze caught one child's and carried it to the centre where it was battered and drowned beneath the fountain. Ella wandered on towards the roundabouts, watched kids on the horses reaching for the brass rings held out by the madame in charge, hooking them onto their sticks, missing them – lively voices shouting one to another – happy.

'Got one!'

'Got three!'

'Five ... ah! Lost it.'

'*Maman!* Again! Again!' And the old woman, taking their money, giving them their wands, setting them off, once again, and the sun shining through the trees which were just coming into leaf but still looking sadly like amputees after the previous autumn's hard pruning: the knobbly stumps reaching up to the sky.

She paused to peek through the fencing of the marionette theatre. It was here that she first sensed that she was being followed. It was nothing unusual: a young girl in Paris was always under the watchful eyes of predatory males, but she was surprised not to have been accosted. Instead, whoever it was, appeared to gain pleasure from the pursuit, and kept himself at a distance, bobbing behind bushes and trees, turning his back, rather than coming out into the open and telling her exactly what he wanted:

'Lady like a bit of jiggy-jiggy?'

She walked onwards, towards the Champs-Elysées, turning round occasionally, but in the mêlée of people, she couldn't see whether she was still being pursued. Deciding on a coffee, she went into the George V and sat down at one of the tables on the *terrasse*, close to the window to watch the world go by: smart, well-coiffured women with their little dogs; business men; tourists; teenagers in denims; friends and couples meeting, shaking hands, kissing, laughing.

It is odd how she could sense that she was the subject of regard. She could tell that someone was looking at her, but when she turned, glancing round from table to table, and then back beyond the aproned waiters, everyone was busy with their own affairs, or engrossed in newspapers (full of the terror of Vietnam) and *livres de poche*. No one was interested in this young girl, alone. And yet, someone was looking at her.

Later on, she went to the cinema to see *Bonnie and Clyde*, English with sub-titles. She had to change her seat several times, and once almost cried out when, engrossed in the film, she bent to scratch a tickle on her bare leg and caught hold of a hand. When she left the cinema, with that familiar feeling of inhabiting two worlds and not sure which was the real, it was already dark and the lights were on: to her left the swirl of Concorde, and beyond that the little arch, and to her right – way up the Champs-Elysées – to Etoile and the massive Arc de Triomphe. It was going home time for many, but for just as many more it was meeting up for an evening out. She thought of Alain, and of the hopelessness of their relationship, imagined having arranged to meet him at Etoile, perhaps, after work, for both, and his coming towards her, raincoat hooked over his finger, slung across his shoulders, pausing to light his cigarette, cupping his hand to shield the flame, inhaling, then the slow drift of smoke across this grey image of dreams.

Walking westwards, pausing to look in a stylish boutique, she saw her own reflection and that of a man lighting a cigarette. He shook the match, drew on the cigarette, looked into her reflected eyes. She turned. He, too, had turned. Just a man in the street, walking away in the opposite direction. Imagination? As she continued, he was there again, and she sensed, if not heard, his footsteps, separated out from all the other tap-tappings and shufflings. In the press of people he was behind her. She looked into windows, stopped, he stopped, stood there, pretending to be engrossed in some display. She dodged into Prisunic, always open at this time, and, yes, as she pushed the glass door, she saw that he was watching, following, as she hurried down the steps to the basement, saw him standing at the top of the steps, he scanning the lower ground floor, she hiding behind a pillar, then running back up the other stairs and out into the street. She was swept along towards the busy crossings of Concorde, and with the push of crowds was gulped down into the digestive system of the Paris Métro and then onto the suburban overland rail.

The small station of Montesson-la-Forêt had a tunnel beneath the railway line. Few people got off, but she was still conscious of a damp veil of fear, so that as she walked through the tunnel, then up the badly lit roadway leading to the house and up to the forest, she kept looking behind her. Other passengers went off along the main road. The house was in darkness, and it was only then she remembered that Madeleine had told her that they would not hurry back, and that she should get something to eat in Paris and catch a late train. Ella had never been given a house-key, and earlier in the day, in the morning sunshine when they'd left, she'd forgotten to ask for one. Occasionally, they hid one under a plant pot to the left of the mailbox, but when she lifted it and felt about in the gravel, there was nothing there. Cold, she sat down on the step before the door and stared out into the darkness. The only window open was that of Madame Vinelli's 'closet,' a narrow space to climb through, but reachable if she got up onto the dustbin. She levered herself onto the sill and clambered in, feet-first, hoping to God she wouldn't put her foot down into the bowl. She did it, quite easily, and slid to the floor, pausing to clamp her hand over her nose.

After having turned on light after light, it was when she had gone into the bedroom to take off her coat that the banging started: thump, thump on the back door. Her first thought was that the family had returned, and she walked out into the hall. The large shape of a man was visible against the frosted glass, and she pressed herself back against the wall, not sure whether he could have seen her. An indistinct face was close to the glass, trying to peer in, a hand above the space for eyes. She scarcely breathed. She wanted to cough. Her eyes filled with the effort of holding back the slightest noise. The fist rapped on the door.

'Is there anyone there?' And she thought the voice familiar and then, no, she just wanted it to be familiar. She listened. She could see the shape step back. It must have banged against the dustbin. There was a loud bump and then a curse.

The outside door – the one into the cellar. She hadn't thought of that. It was always being left open. That was where he was going. That was it. He knew it was open. She tried to close the door at the top of the cellar steps – that's the way to lock him out. The rusty bolts wouldn't budge. Down the steps and the lamp from the hallway casting a meagre light. The light switch over by the garden door which was – now she was quite certain – open and ready for that shape to get in. And once in the cellar having to grope her way across the stone-flagged floor, knowing that so much rubble, bottles and garden equipment, was always left lying about. The crack in the door gave her an indistinct marker and she had to get there before he did.

Her scream was so loud that it terrified her, as if it was sounding all round her, coming out of the walls and not from her at all. And then it was as if her breath simply stopped, as if the long, long cry had emptied her lungs of air and she couldn't breathe – there was no strength to take in new air – and something big and heavy, hanging there, swinging in front of her, a weight, warm, it had felt warm – swinging. Instead of moving away, she moved towards it and kicked something at her feet which splashed over onto her ankles.

'Little English girl?' The light clicked on as the garden door opened. She looked down at her feet and they were covered with blood, and then the heavy body swinging, headless, its legs stretched up and tied to a huge hook.

Once started, she couldn't stop laughing, hysterical laughing. 'My God! You've killed him!' and the tears were streaming down her cheeks as she pointed towards the headless bird, the blood continuing to drip into a chipped enamel bowl.

'Chopped its head off,' said Philippe Gravelin. 'I told them I'd do it for them while they're away. Get it done.' He was holding a large curved knife, and he slashed through the air with it. 'Single stroke. Like that. Like that.'

'The poor, poor old turkey.' She looked down at the blood, still gently rocking in the bowl.

'He wasn't old. He's a good bird,' and he looked at her. 'I was knocking at the door.'

'I didn't hear.'

'No? I called out.'

'I thought I'd heard something and I came to look.'

He glanced away, shrugged, then turned back to stare at her, doubtfully. 'Well then,' he looked at the bird. 'We'll eat that next Sunday. Easter dinner.' He saw her eyeing the knife in his hand and moved towards her. She instinctively backed away, and could feel the blood already drying on her bare skin. 'Are you afraid, little English girl? Why are you afraid? Afraid of me?' And the smile – and the knife.

She heard the sound of a car. 'They're home,' she said. 'They're home again!'

VII

She beckoned to Ella from the doorway of her bedroom. In her nightdress, a fluffy pink dressing-gown over her shoulders, flat slippers, in place of her usual high heels, Madame Vinelli looked surprisingly small and vulnerable. She had removed her makeup – even her glasses – and her hair was covered by a pink chiffon tied in a bow on top of her head. Ella had been on her way up to the bathroom. She put her sponge-bag and towel down on the table at the front door, where Saint Theresa looked mournfully down at them, as if seeking for her lost nose.

'What is it? What d'you want? Are you ill?'

She just beckoned again, shaking her head to show that they should make no noise. Ella followed her into the bedroom, pulling the door to behind her. Madame Vinelli indicated a chair, one of the threadbare Louis Quinze, while she herself sat down on the larger chair beside the bed, the photograph of Captain Luigi just visible behind her.

It was the evening of Easter Sunday, 14th April, and a great deal had happened during the day. Madame Vinelli had been enclosed in her room since leaving the dining-room in angry tears. Ella hadn't been able to follow exactly what the row had been about, but now she wondered whether she was in for dismissal, perhaps without any reference to Monsieur and Madame Tessier, perhaps on their behalf, perhaps because of her involvement in their marriage, perhaps because of none of these. 'Adultery' and 'abortion,' were these going to be given a thorough airing? Her mind turned to Captain Luigi Vinelli and to the photograph beneath his own. If only he knew who was tucked behind his haughty portrait! She glanced at the bedspread, as if it might still reveal having been sat upon, providing evidence of her own meddling, and then again at the Vinelli smile. She imagined the fragility of the little tin clip keeping the dreadful secret in place, but hardly secure.

When Madame Vinelli began to speak, it was with some difficulty. The words came out in little bursts, as if she was too upset to let them go. They were ejected like water from the garden pump, before it had begun to flow freely. Plop – the water splashed into the bucket, and Madame's words were given in hesitant, incomplete sentences. After a while, Ella realized that they had something to do with adultery, but it was going to require a good bit of pumping before that deep, deep sin would emerge. And abortion? Well, in a way, with a bit of lateral thinking, that too was swimming murkily in the depths.

'It is unforgivable what Alain's done. I shall never forgive him. Never.' she said.

Ella listened – waited.

'I suppose he's known for a long time. But who told him?' Another pause.

Ella leant forwards, uncertain. The woman was speaking so slowly. Had she taken her teeth out? It wasn't too easy to make out the words; there was a lot of noise at the back of the throat and Ella's command of French was being seriously tested.

'I think I know who it was.' She had been looking down at her hands but now she raised her eyes to Ella. Without her glasses, those eyes looked pink and watery, and with the white nightdress and pink Orlon dressing-gown, Ella was reminded of a white rabbit. She thought of the time that must be spent each morning getting that face ready to start the day. Still she didn't know what it was all about, so still she said nothing. Inadvertently she once again glanced beyond the older woman to that photograph, and seeing the direction of her gaze, Madame Vinelli turned and picked it up, pressing her lips against the glass. Another pair of red mating slugs.

'Now it's coming,' thought Ella 'Now I'm for it.'

'It was a long time ago.' The water, the words, began

to flow freely, all of a sudden the blockage had been released and it came out in a rush. Ella sat back. 'Of course it was, and things were very different then. You can't know what it was like. Careful, you had to be so careful. Having them here, the Germans – I mean they were walking down the street – not so many here, in this area out of Paris, but they came here – in the bars, drinking, our place ...,' and she stopped for a moment, lowering her voice, as if her long dead mother might be listening. 'That's what my mother used to say – you'd think they owned the place – and they did, I mean – own the place. Of course you don't know. What does it mean to you? You're still just a child.'

Ella continued to stare silently at the woman, wondering how much she could see without her glasses. Perhaps to this older woman's pale eyes, in the dim light, she was just a swimming shape. She yawned. It had nothing to do with her. She was tired and wanted to get to bed. Madame Vinelli was gazing down at the face of her husband who had died so long ago.

'Oh!' said Ella, caught mid-yawn, as the grandmother turned over the frame, staring at the back for what seemed to the girl an incredibly long time. But without saying anything more, the long red fingernails picked under the remaining tin fastening, bending it back too far, just as Ella had done – the final one – so that it snapped and fell to the floor. They both looked down at the parquet, Madame Vinelli tutting in irritation. She continued to unpack the secret, sliding out the card backing, then the thin sheets of tissue paper that served as padding, then the photograph of the young man with blonde hair and a boyish grin, a personality very different from Luigi. Ella didn't need to see it, but even so, she bent over and held out her hands. Before passing it to her, the older woman drew back.

'So,' thought Ella, 'not me. Nothing to do with me,' and she felt relieved, and slightly guilty at having wanted another's worries to lessen her own.

'Don't you want to know?' Madame Vinelli stood up. She still held the glass and silver frame, but Luigi's photograph had slipped to the floor, and Ella noticed that the slippered feet had almost stepped on it. Despite herself, she smiled at the heavy but unintentional symbolism and thought that there are times when real life does out-do the intricacies of art. She took the small photo and reminded herself of what was written across the smiling face.

'D'you understand what I've given you – what you're holding?'

Ella frowned and handed it back.

Madame Vinelli explained how she had continued to live with her mother at *La Fauvette*, after her husband had returned to Italy to do his duty for his own country.

'Anyway, he couldn't stay here. An enemy now. Suddenly all changed – that's what happens in war, though you wouldn't know.' She nodded her head sharply. That was that, the way things were and are in wartime. Understand? You understand? Huh?'

He'd gone back. She'd been left alone with her mother and then France was occupied and she was just a young woman caught up in it all, like everyone else, and you kept your head down and got on with things as best you could – as best anyone could.

'And you don't know what it is to be afraid. I mean really afraid. You've got to get on. On. Nod to them there in the street – ah! *Bonjour* – and they – *Messieurs Dames* – polite, it's like that, in the war. Interlopers. You meet them – try not to meet them, but you meet them – in their boots. And you didn't open your doors at night. Mind you, you know, some people ... Humph! All in the past, they say now, and we don't want to rake over all that.'

She went on and on, and Ella looked longingly towards the door and thought of bed. She talked about her loneliness, just with her mother. You made do. Digging, growing as much as you could. Giving some to the Germans, on the safe side. But there weren't that many round here, they did come, of course. Oh yes, don't think that they didn't come – not a nuisance, watched their manners, on the whole. And then – and she sank back in the chair. She must be tiring, Ella thought, and amused herself by making comparisons with furnishings and food: Madame Vinelli was a pastel cushion leant upon too long; a pink and white ice-cream, strawberry and vanilla, beginning to melt; disintegrating meringue.

She was off again. Ella shuffled her feet. It was one day, she said, when she had gone up to the spring to fetch the water. No car, of course, they didn't have the petrol or the cars. She had walked up, pulling her little handcart behind her, to get the water – yes, yes, she prevented Ella from interrupting – her little cart with a rope, to bring back the water as they'd always done. And she'd got to the spring – to the spring – and waited for her turn.

'It wasn't as organized as it is now,' she said. 'Not at all. You didn't have the pipe. There was a table, not the one that's there now. It was an old thing with not enough room on it to put your bottles. I didn't use bottles. I had this big container, sometimes two, they were my father's. When full, they were heavy to lift, and this time, this day, there was a young German and he'd stopped by for a drink, I suppose, but when I tried to lift them onto the cart, he helped me. He wanted to pull it home for me, but I said no. But he did, all the same, when he saw me with it running away down the hill! It was heavy, you see, especially when I had two of the containers, and I'd two that day.' She smiled, remembering. She didn't seem to be thinking about Ella.

'No, I'd said no. I said that I could manage. After all, I didn't want help from a German, and I didn't want anyone seeing me getting help from him. But he just took the rope from me and pulled it home – just the same.'

Ella smiled, too.

'He just took the rope handle from me, and I walked beside him. I didn't say anything – not a word – except *merci, merci bien, Monsieur.*'

She was still sitting back in the chair, and Ella thought of her less as a rabbit, cushion or parti-coloured ice-cream, and more as she once was, young, probably beautiful, like her daughter.

And, as if the woman understood what she was thinking, she said, 'I had long dark hair, not blonde like now. Small, I was, *petite*, light-boned, you'd say. He was around after that – but always careful. I'd see him in the lane, and at the spring, he was often there, on the edge of the forest. Not everyone spoke to him – some turned their eyes away. I mean, Monsieur Bombert, for example, he used to live down the hill, on the other corner, opposite Monsieur Fontenay's place, when he saw any of them he just turned round and went straight home. They didn't like that. It wasn't polite.' She looked straight at Ella. 'That's what it was like, though. And it was the uniform.' She stopped and thought for a few seconds. 'Oh he was a good-looking young man, a bit of a boy, really. I was twenty-five and he was only twenty-two. Much younger than Luigi.'

She nodded, sat up, as if she'd finished all she'd got to say. Ella began to stand up. Was this it? It wasn't. She sat down again.

'There were walks in the forest. Not near the spring where anyone might see.' Ella turned away, suddenly seeing herself and Alain, alone in the forest. 'There used to be a small stone building, half-ruined. I never knew what it was. Animals, I suppose. There was some firewood and piles of straw. It didn't smell nice. It belonged to the Gravelin family.'

'Monsieur Philippe Gravelin?'

'His family. He's alone now, of course. Then, he was a young man. His father'd died, but grandparents, brother and three cousins, and his mother. He was my age and fond of me,' she surprised Ella with a wink. 'Always in the forest, even then. Always lighting fires – and hunting.'

'One night – it was winter, there was plenty of snow. Sometimes he would write to me. I've kept the letters,' she nodded over to the little cabinet. Ella didn't look. 'I told my mother that they came from an old schoolfriend. He couldn't always come to Montesson, less and less often really, but he'd write when he would be coming.' There was a silence. Ella waited, interested now. 'He'd asked me to meet him – this night, the one I'm talking about – near the spring. It was dark and there was very little lighting. You didn't go out in the dark, you closed the shutters and put up the boards. I took a small torch and told Maman that I was going up to the Gravelins' – Madame Gravelin had been ill, you see. Maman didn't want me to go, but I set off just the same. I was willful! I put on my best boots, black leather bootees – belonging to Maman – with a little heel and a cuff of imitation Persian lamb that folded over at the ankle and fastened with a silver button. Lovely boots. It was hard to walk in the snow in the little high-heels.'

She paused and smiled, as if seeing herself all over again: and the lane; and the snow; and she walking up to the spring – slipping in the snow; and the water at the spring, frozen; she shining her torch on the icicles hanging down around the edges, great long ones, glinting in the light of her torch – in the light of his torch. He'd snapped one off, pretending it was a dagger, and then he'd put the point into his mouth, shouted at the cold, and then he'd put it in her mouth, this long shaft of ice.

Madame Vinelli pulled the pink dressing-gown round her shoulders, as if again experiencing the cold of that night – and the icicles.

'It began to snow. Soft, slow, white flakes, at first, then more and more. He had a thick army greatcoat on and he took it off and wrapped it round me.'

Ella nodded, thinking of that night with Alain, snuggled beneath his heavy greatcoat, and then she thought how they, too, had lain like babes in the wood beneath that coat, in the cold.

'It was so dark and we could hardly see each other in

the sheet of snow, even when I shone my torch. Just a sheet of snow. So strange in the dark, by the light of our torches. He set off ahead of me – he didn't know where he was walking and I'm sure it must have been luck that brought us to the old stone ruin. I shone the torch on the ground and lit up his deep imprints – placing ...' and her hands gently patted the air, one hand in front of the other, 'my little feet in their little black bootees, then one, then the other.' She spread her fingers and continued to pat the air. 'My feet in the deep hollows made by his big army boots. I trod in his steps – following – taking great big strides, so that once I nearly toppled over, and then I did fall, and we laughed and he picked me up and carried me into the place – you can still see the stones of the foundations – and we sheltered from the snow.' There was a long silence.

After what had seemed a very long time, she turned her face to Ella. 'Five months later, I went to stay with an aunt and cousin, near Rouen, and I stayed there until the end of the war, and then I came home with the little Madeleine.'

Ella didn't know whether to speak, she didn't want to say anything to break the strange stillness that had wrapped around them. For a moment, they sat motionless, just looking at each other, and with the understanding of two women who knew what it was like to fall in love, to fall for an ideal of love – perhaps – with the romance of it all, and the secret, illicit love – and for a short time an absence of all the obligations imposed by the hard world beyond.

Finally, Ella spoke, and very quietly. 'And he?'

'Disappeared. I expect that he was sent somewhere else. Wartime, you never know what's coming. Disappeared – just disappeared – and I never had the chance to tell him.'

'And Captain Vinelli? Your reaching the Italian border? You went all that way?'

'No. Never. I was told about his murder – no details. They just said the communists. And then I was someone to be pitied and it was perfectly acceptable to see this little girl as his. But if anyone had known the truth, what wouldn't they have done to me?' Her eyes were full of fear and her hands were gripping the chipped, gilded arms of the chair. Ella realized why she was so frightened of the law, as if one day this guilty secret of fraternization with the enemy might be made known. Her daughter's real father would become public knowledge.

'The shame,' she said.

'But even after all these years?'

'Of course.' And there followed another long silence, but now, Ella didn't think of longing for sleep, but of the awful consequences of what she had been told. Could this still be kept secret from Madeleine?

Madame Vinelli has started again, speaking slowly and hesitantly, as she had done at the start. 'They say it's all in the past and that we don't need to look back. As if we can put it behind us. But it's all still there. Just beneath the surface, peel it back.' And she held out a hand, and moved her fingers, finger and thumb, as if picking at the corner of a sheet of paper. The fingers became claw-like, wrenching at the air, as at a heavy blanket or the edge of a thick greatcoat. She tugged at the weight of the coat.

'You might say I was unlucky. Only once – once, and the very first time.'

Ella nodded, and thought of her very first time. Lucky? Was it that?

The older woman sank back in the chair, breathing deeply. 'Well I don't see it as unlucky. I have Madeleine and all my sorrow is that she married *him*.'

How strange for Ella to have her love, or rather her loved one, dismissed as of no worth; the hatred directed against him by this woman was so intense. Politics, aesthetics – 'he's such an ugly man,' she'd said – or something unexplained within the man himself? Was it that she had long suspected that he had known the truth of all this for some time, was that what lay behind this detestation? And he, did he resent the fact that she had kept it secret and had not been able to face up to the cruelty, the real cruelty, that would have been meted out to her? Perhaps this was it, who could say?

'Of course, Philippe Gravelin had been in love with me. And later, much later – he fell for Madeleine – pursued her.' She stopped and looked directly at Ella. 'His house is on the edge of the forest, close by the foundations of the old stone building.'

Ella nodded.

'He hunts in all weathers – in all weathers,' said Madame Vinelli. She looked towards the clock above the bed, beside the crucifix. 'And now you must go to bed. Good night and sleep well, Ella.'

But Ella did not sleep well, in fact, she tossed and turned, unable to get out of her mind all that had taken place that day. Late in the night, she thought that she had heard the cellar door open and close, and the sound of footsteps across the hall. She certainly had heard raised voices in the bedroom above, but she had been unable to make out whether they had belonged only to Alain and Madeleine, or whether Charles had also been involved. When it was clear that she was not going to do other than doze, she'd got up, intending to go to the downstairs kitchen to get a drink – of anything she could find. It was cold. On opening the bedroom door, she was surprised to see a faint light coming from the room opposite, the room where they had had dinner. They had had the light on earlier, so perhaps no one had turned it off. She pushed the door open to find Madame Vinelli sitting beside the open window: the shutters had been flung back.

'Oh, Madame Vinelli! How you frightened me there.'

The older woman did not turn, but continued to gaze out into the dark.

'I couldn't sleep,' Ella continued, walking over

towards the window, and clutching her dressing-gown round her shoulders. 'It's freezing in here. You can't sit like this – in such cold.' She stretched out to catch hold of the fastening on the shutters.

'Leave it!' Her voice was brittle.

Ella hesitated before going back to bed. Still she couldn't sleep, she found herself going through the events of the day. She listened for any sound which might indicate that the grandmother had returned to her bedroom, but heard nothing, and in the end, she fell asleep, waking in the morning much later than usual, when Sissy called out to her from her cot in the corner.

Now that Ella had heard Madame Vinelli's story, she was better able to understand why the Easter dinner had ended as it did. The day had started so well, and Philippe Gravelin had arrived early to get the turkey in the oven. There'd been bustling around and laughter, with Sissy running about between them, looking for the little Easter eggs that Ella had bought from the local *pâtisserie* and hidden around the house. Her grandmother had pretended to be angry – 'Sissy, you're always under my feet. Run away and play with your toys somewhere else.' But Ella could tell that beneath the strict exterior, she was happy to have the child with her, and for the family, with Philippe and possibly Charles, to be together. Her cousin, from near Rouen, her aunt's daughter, was coming later in the morning, so there were eight expected round the table. As Philippe cooked the turkey, the grandmother was fussing in her dining-room, seeking out crystal wine glasses and a porcelain plate for the Easter *gâteau*. This cake had been made the previous evening, in order not to interfere with the roasting turkey. For at least a week, possibly longer, before leaving for work, Madame had been diligently skimming off the skin of the boiled milk used for breakfast coffee and for Sissy's hot chocolate, placing it in a pan which was kept outside on the kitchen window ledge (there was no refrigerator). The accumulated yellow soured cream was then used for the cake.

Charles Fontenay had promised to come, but his arrival was always unpredictable, and, in fact, he turned up at the last minute, when all of them were already seated at the table in the ground-floor dining-room. Alain had gone earlier in the morning to fetch the cheese and salad from the market. Madeleine, as usual, stayed in bed until all was ready, and then descended, dressed attractively in a lavender dress which almost matched her platinum hair rinse. She was carrying a pile of records to play on the old record player.

'Good morning to you all,' she smiled sweetly, and just at that moment her cousin from Rouen, Madame Marie Laval, arrived with more chocolate eggs for Sissy and another *gâteau*. Madame Vinelli eyed the second cake with pursed lips, thanked her cousin, kissed her profusely, and placed the offending cake on an upper shelf in the kitchen. Ella was introduced to the cousin, an elderly lady, who must have been at least ten years older than Madame Vinelli. Alain poured aperitifs for everyone:

'Cinzano, Marie? And you, too, Marguerite? Ella? Madeleine?'

'*Salut!*' and they raised their glasses, listening to Philippe in the kitchen.

'It's the turkey, Marie. You remember the one at the bottom of the garden? We should've had him for Christmas but he was a bit too small.'

'My turkey?' said Sissy.

'But, of course, my little one. Your very own and Uncle Philippe is preparing it for dinner.'

It was three o'clock when they all eventually sat down to eat, shifting the chairs round to squeeze in another when Charles arrived. Ella put Sissy's high chair at the top of the table.

'Charles, I didn't think that you were going to make it,' and Alain went in search of another chair. 'Where will you sit? Here, next to me? Ah, beside Madeleine. *Voilà!* That's it. Superb.'

'And what book are you working on now?' Madame Marie Laval leant towards him. 'I read your last one – your best, I think.'

'Now that would be telling and I never reveal anything prior to publication. But, rest assured, you'll all be in it – just as you are.' Everyone laughed.

Madame Vinelli beamed round the table. 'Alain,' she said. 'Would you cut the bread? Give a little piece for Sissy to use as a pusher. You want the crusty end, my little one? Of course you do. Alain! The bread, if you please.'

As soon as everyone had been served with turkey, Madeleine got up to choose a record. 'Ray Charles? Yes?'

The conversation continued to be lively, and Ella struggled to keep up with its twists and turns. Charles was on his usual good form, full of the student unrest in Nanterre and Paris. He wanted to know what Alain thought about its spreading into the capital, and whether anyone thought it likely to get out of hand. He'd read a number of pessimistic pieces in the newspapers and now he wanted something from the horse's mouth, as it were.

'Now you're on the inside, Alain, so spill the beans.'

'Oh, do. Yes!' said Madame Laval, who loved a bit of gossip. Madame Vinelli said that she was exasperated with it all and that the young nowadays just wanted everything, simply everything. She blamed the influence of America, the films – all American. And the language so full of Americanisms. Could one blame the young for acting as they did? Madeleine said that she also felt that America was a corrupting influence. Madame Laval asked Ella what she thought, since this was her mother tongue. Ella explained that she was not American and that the English and American cultures were, in many ways, quite different, but yes, she, too, agreed that the spread of American influence was worrying and threatened to obliterate obvious and more subtle differences between cultures across Europe.

Charles brought the conversation back to the students, asking whether Alain and Philippe thought it possible that the workers could become further involved in the disturbances. Did he believe that so many divergent sources of protest could be drawn together under one umbrella, if he could usefully employ that metaphor? Alain ran a finger over his upper lip, concentrating upon what was being said.

'In my opinion, it's by no means impossible that this –' he paused, 'this turbulence could escalate and become even more worrying. I mean, I have to say that already they are fully occupying the University authorities. We've already had to close down Nanterre for a short period – yes, things got *that* bad. What you don't want, what nobody wants, is too forceful a response from the government – should the riot police be brought in – a disaster! The students have got a lot of justifiable complaints, and any response that appears to be treating them – the students – as undisciplined children, could fire an even more serious revolt. You know, this may seem to have risen from nowhere, but it has a history – things have been warming, simmering, for quite a while.'

'Well, of course,' said his mother-in-law, 'we know you're on their side.' Alain didn't answer. Madeleine got up and put on another record.

'Jacques Brel?' she asked.

'As you will,' replied her mother, tartly, still looking at Alain.

'Well,' said Philippe, 'personally, I suspect it'll all fizzle out. These things do. Unless they have the workers on their side – and unless they get the unions with them, and they're dead against, I think. Got their eyes on future power!'

'Exactly,' said Madame Vinelli, and her cousin nodded in agreement. 'The young, they get these ideas, but youthful exuberance burns brightly and is soon extinguished. It's an extreme nuisance, though. Madeleine and I've stopped going anywhere near the left bank on Saturdays.'

Madeleine looked towards her husband, who had become exceptionally quiet. He leant back and raised his glass:

'*Santé*. To the revolution!' winking towards his mother-in-law, intent upon irritating her.

'*Ah, non!* That's not possible.' Madeleine wagged a finger across the table. 'Student rioting is one thing, revolution quite another.'

'Madeleine's right,' said Charles. 'You overstate the severity of the situation. Retract that last comment, Alain. Pure mischief.' But, as usual, Charles ended by laughing.

'Well, maybe.' Alain cut himself another slice of turkey. 'But I'm not alone in thinking this more worrying that any of us first imagined. Listen Charles, you're right to talk about worker unrest and students' attempts to bring them into the dispute. Don't underestimate the student body, my friends – my comrades' (that deliberately inserted to annoy his wife's mother), 'don't underestimate their power. They could become something to be reckoned with. They've got international support – some of them forever crossing frontiers. There's plenty ready to latch onto any unrest, no matter what. Some of them have no idea what they're joining – individual irritations just gather round. Idealistic, they may be, but with some – with many – their ideals are good – they know what they're doing. Others just attach themselves like burrs to whatever's going – don't necessarily understand what they're fighting for! But this sort of undirected support can still provide the energy, the fuel. No, comrades' (Madame Vinelli frowned at him) 'don't be too ready to dismiss them.' Again, he raised his glass to the revolution. And for good measure, he hummed the *Internationale*.

Charles and Philippe, Philippe more reluctantly, clinked their glasses. From the old record player, Jacques Brel's rousing, anti-bourgeois lyrics gave further weight to the sentiments expressed. Philippe glanced towards Madeleine.

'To the revolution?' she said, raising her eyebrows. 'At

any rate, I'll drink to a new and better world. To liberty.' She stretched forward her glass towards Philippe and laughed. Charles watched them, glass still poised, but after a second's silence, he threw back his head and said:

'To Madeleine – and her beauty.'

'To Madeleine,' Philippe said more softly. 'To my own Madeleine.'

Alain was at the end of the table. He looked at the two men, looked from one to the other, and with a slight smile said, 'Yes, of course, yes. To the beautiful Madeleine – and to Ella.' They raised their glasses to Ella, who had been sitting quietly, watching.

'To the English girl,' said Philippe Gravelin.

She smiled in recognition. 'To Madame Vinelli and Madame Laval,' she said, 'and to *their* beauty.' The two older women looked slightly embarrassed.

Course followed course, wine followed wine. At the end of the meal, Madame Vinelli brought in the Easter *gâteau*. Her cousin noted that it was not the one she had brought, but said nothing. Madeleine went over to kiss her mother:

'Maman, that looks delicious. Alain, thank Maman.'

'Marguerite, you've excelled yourself. Magnificent.'

Each took a slice, Charles excusing himself from too large a portion, whilst Philippe made up for it with his huge chunk.

'*Mamie. S'il te plaît,*' asked Sissy, from her high chair at the other end of the table.

'Of course, my little one,' and her grandmother gave her the last slice, picking out one of the cherries from her own serving and placing it on top of the child's. 'It was Luigi's favourite. Luigi my husband,' she explained to Ella. The last record had finished and Philippe leant over and lifted the needle. He looked through the record sleeves. 'My husband,' continued Marguerite Vinelli, 'holds a special place in my heart.' The table fell silent. Alain and Madeleine looked down at their plates.

'Yes, well,' said Alain. 'And who's for a little coffee?'

Madame Vinelli gestured to him to be quiet. 'Just for a moment. I was speaking of my husband. Just a moment, please.'

Alain closed his eyes and clasped his hands before him, resigned to what he, and the others, expected to follow. And sure enough, the older woman began, all over again, the story of her flight through occupied France to meet her husband and conceive her child.

It was well past the time for Sissy's afternoon nap, and after having fought off sleep throughout the final part of the meal, the child had slumped forward in her high-chair. Ella picked her up, with help from Charles, and took her through to the bedroom to pop her into her cot. She waited a while to make sure that she didn't wake up.

When she returned to the dining-room, a violent row had broken out. Charles was standing, as if intending to leave. Philippe was leaning back, his chair balanced on two legs, observing the scene with an amused smile.

'You could never have made that journey by yourself – highly unlikely that you did.' This was Alain.

'How dare you question my integrity.' This was Madame Vinelli.

'Yes, Alain. How can you suggest that Maman is lying?'

'I just state the truth, as I perceive it. I state what I know to be fact and what I think to be probable. You forget Madeleine, you forget Marguerite,' turning from one to the other, 'that I have made a study of this time – an aspect of my life's work. I respect what my own research suggests. No!' he raised his hand to silence the two women.

Charles Fontenay left and let himself out of the house. Philippe Gravelin stood up, still smiling and seeming to enjoy the argument.

Alain continued. 'I suggest, Marguerite, that your memory plays you false. Marie,' he turned to her cousin, 'after all, she came to live with your mother and you for the rest of the war.'

Madame Laval had been sitting very still, but now she looked directly at her cousin. 'Marguerite, I really don't understand what all this is about, but I think you ought to tell them. Tell them how it was. It's so long ago. What does it matter now? Madeleine needs to know. She should know.' She lowered her voice. 'You can't sit on it forever.'

Madame Vinelli pushed back her chair. 'Marie, this is nothing to do with you, and I'm sorry that you have had to witness it all.' She turned to Alain. 'May I remind you, Monsieur Tessier, that you live here, under my roof, at my invitation. It is I who tolerate you, not the other way about. May I remind you, Monsieur Tessier, that my husband fought – and died – for his country.' She left the room, only to return two minutes later to hiss through the door. 'You are not fit to polish his boots. Filthy communist.'

Ella and Madeleine cleared the table, the coffee abandoned. Philippe Gravelin stayed to listen to the remains of the fracas. Madeleine went back and forth between kitchen and dining-room, and each time she entered the latter, where her husband, his friend, and her mother's bemused cousin, were still sitting, she launched another burst of abuse towards the man who had, she said, sullied her father's memory, had abused her mother's generosity, had ruined her own marriage. She didn't know how he could live in this house and show such ingratitude. She didn't know how he could live at all. She wished that he were dead.

VIII

To find that her father, whose photograph she had been shown throughout her life, wasn't her natural father, was hard to bear. She had lived with the image of a man she had never in reality seen. He had been presented to her as an heroic figure, a father who merited her pride. That she was attracted towards and was an attraction for older men must surely have had more than a little to do with the absence of her father, who had existed always as a black and white photograph from a silent past.

She had learnt to speak Italian in memory of this man, although, surprisingly, she had never been to Italy. Madeleine would not accept what she was now told about a father, who had not only disappeared but had been one of the occupying enemy: blond where he was dark; quite small where he was tall; young and boyish in appearance and very far, in her imagination, from that superior Italian face with its thick eyebrows and aquiline nose.

The fact that Alain had brought this past into the open made him, she decided, an associate of this German usurper – this imposter. She could not believe and she would not believe it to be true. Her own father, whose image she had held dear, had been killed. This other had deserted his lover and his child – whether he knew of the expected child was of no consequence to Madeleine, none at all.

And yet, there was something about this myth, for she struggled to see it as anything other than a mythical tale (a fairy story that her mother had felt impelled to create, for some unknown reason), which deep down inside her made a kind of sense of her life. It was as if something within her had known that the emptiness was not being properly filled by the grainy photographs she was shown. As if, in some part of her brain, she had always experienced a searching after something unattainable. This, at any rate, is what she told herself when she had overcome her first adamant denial and begun the attempt to disentangle all that she had been told.

Her mother showed her photographs, not many, not many at all, of herself as a young woman. There she was, in a tiny square, black and white photograph with crinkly edges, standing at the bottom of the garden of *La Fauvette*, smiling, her hands holding branches of apple blossom cut from trees by the chicken run. In those days there had been a small orchard. There she was on her wedding day, serious, her hand resting on the arm of the tall Italian Madeleine knew as her father. And there she was, a small figure in a dark coat, strapped shoes, hair pulled back from her forehead, on the step at the back of the house, looking out into the empty lane, alone. Madeleine picked up the small glossy squares, now browning with age, depicting the young man they said was her true father. He was wearing his German uniform – smiling – his hands in his pockets, a cigarette in the corner of his mouth. He meant nothing to her.

It seemed to her that Alain had destroyed her father twice over. Because of him, she now had this stranger. Alain's left-wing sympathies linked him in her mind with the partisans, the communists who, according to her mother, had murdered the man she took to be her papa. His death had been part of the settling of scores at the end of the war.

She placed the photographs back into the box in which they had been given to her and thought of burning the lot. But they didn't belong to her, not her memories, they were her mother's past, nothing, she felt now, belonged to her.

She didn't want comfort. She didn't want anything to do with Sissy. Ella looked after the child, and her grandmother took over when she came from work. But it couldn't go on like that. Ella wanted to get away, but she couldn't leave this little girl alone with Madeleine, for

Madeleine was not herself. The nerves so much lived upon were thoroughly exhausted.

And what of Alain? And what of Charles? After that Easter dinner, Charles had retreated and it seemed that he must have gone away on one of his escapades, for Madeleine wrote to him, again and again, giving her letters to Philippe Gravelin, who probably never delivered any of them, because she never received any reply. She rang the bell outside the iron gate of his house, tugging hard on the chain, and there was no response.

Alain left the house and slept on the truckle-bed at the University; he was increasingly caught up with the activities of the students.

Things were not good. It was Madame Vinelli who asked her cousin Marie Laval whether she would take Sissy for a while, just until something could be sorted, until they could reconcile Madeleine to her responsibilities: these were Madame Vinelli's sentiments, and for her there was no recognition of the part she had played in alienating her son-in-law.

Once Sissy had gone and Ella had packed up some of her toys and extra clothing, to be forwarded later, there was really no reason for her to remain. But remain she did – for a while, at any rate – and the fact that she did was to make her a witness to and a part of something she would remember for the rest of her life.

It was on Sunday 5th May that Alain Tessier returned to *La Fauvette* and found Ella sitting in the garden in the sunshine. He had been home briefly on other occasions after that Easter Sunday, but this was the first time since Sissy had left.

Ella had heard the sound of the old Citroën, and she looked up from her book, immediately recognizing the engine. Instinctively she glanced up to the windows of Madeleine's bedroom, but the shutters were partially closed against the sun. Madame Vinelli was in her room at the back of the house, knitting a green cardigan for Sissy. Nobody had questioned Ella about her staying on, they were caught up with their own unhappinesses, and so she was able to come and go as she pleased, sometimes cooking for the two women, sometimes eating alone. The house had an echoing emptiness. Now and again, she went to Paris, but steered clear of the left bank, where students were demonstrating, wielding placards and banners, breaking out into spasmodic fights and surges of serious violence.

On one day, on the Boulevard Montparnasse, she'd been sitting in a café looking out into the busy street, when military police had marched past, and she'd felt a frisson of fear at the sight of guns, helmets and marching men. But so far, she had witnessed little other than scuffles and occasional sightings of rowdy students and grouped police, although she knew well of the massed demonstrations and the strong reactions of the armed force. The newspapers and radio carried full reports on the rising tide of anger and the fears about the way in which the workers were being drawn in. She was careful to avoid the area around the University.

Seated in the garden, she listened for the engine of the Citroën to cut out and watched to see whether Alain would appear. He must have expected her to be out there, or perhaps he was looking for his wife, for he came straight round to the back of the house, carrying his old briefcase, his shirt open at the neck, and walking towards Ella with that slightly stiff gait which had become so familiar to her – so much a part of the man he was. She laid aside her book and felt that old attraction towards him, a fondness now tinged with sympathy. The cat, Myrtille, had been sitting on her lap, and it jumped down as she moved to stand up. She went across the lawn towards him, the cat following her, arching its back and rubbing itself against her legs when she stopped to wait for him to reach her.

'Alain.' He looked tired, even haggard.

'I thought I might find you here, Ella. I phoned the butcher to see whether you'd left. I didn't think that you'd stay – not after Sissy had gone.'

At first, it was an awkward meeting and neither of them knew what to say to each other. She wasn't sure whether his affection towards her had changed: whether, for him, it had been no more than a light affair which shouldn't have happened and now that it had ended should be forgotten. And for herself – well, after all that had taken place, this little flickering of love seemed small fry, as if a long time ago. But, despite herself, she longed to take his arm. Whatever Madame Vinelli might say, she understood how and probably why Madeleine had been drawn towards him. They walked back towards the house in silence. As they moved round the side of the house, shielded from windows and from the lane by trees and shrubs, he stopped and turned towards her, and placing the old briefcase down on the ground, he tipped her face up to his own.

'I suppose you'll be leaving?'

'There's nothing to keep me here – is there? Now that Sissy's gone. I've no idea when they plan to bring her back or how long Madame Laval can keep her.'

'Of course, you must go.' And when Ella heard this, she knew that she'd wanted it to be otherwise. She wanted, unreasonably, the romance with a happy resolution, but she'd always known that it wasn't going to be like that. 'You ought to get out now,' he continued. 'The situation in Paris is getting – ,' and he paused, seeking for the correct word, 'dangerous, very dangerous. I have to warn you. Paris is not, and will not be the best place to be. It's getting increasingly difficult to contain, and you never know which way it's going to turn. Get out, while you can.'

'While I can,' and she laughed. 'This is extreme talk.'

'Maybe. Maybe. But it's for an extreme state. I've never seen anything like this. They talk of the past and revolution in the blood.'

'Oh, Alain!' and again she laughed, but this time with rather less conviction. 'You're not being serious – are you serious?'

'Yes. Yes I am,' he turned, shaking his head. 'I'll have to go in and see Madeleine. D'you want me to tell her you're leaving?'

'No, not yet. I'll tell her myself when I've sorted things out in my mind. Anyway, I'll have to book my flight. There's no point bothering her when she's not well.'

'Is she ill? I didn't know or I'd have come before.'

'It's been a shock for her and I think she feels that she's no one to turn to. She needs your help.'

'I suppose that this is the end for us, Ella.' He placed his hand on the back of her neck, and she turned to him and smiled.

'I suppose it is. It's been a short – affair.' She looked up and kissed him.

'But a happy one?'

'I don't know about that,' she laughed. 'I've done a bit of growing up!'

'What about a day or two together in Paris – next week? Just to say goodbye – to give our brief affair an ending.'

'Like all good affairs, close it one way or another?'

'That's it. And I'm lonely, you know, in Paris by myself.'

'What a lie! You're never alone. You're surrounded by students, friends – comrades in the cause. But Paris? After all you've said.' She laughed loudly and kissed him playfully on the cheek. 'What an old rascal you are,' she thought, 'but what a likeable one.' Then aloud – 'It'll certainly spice up the end of my adventure.'

'I'll take care of you. Haven't I always?'

'Well ...! I'll try to get a plane for Saturday 11th May.'

'That could be difficult – to get a flight on a Saturday? Maybe not.'

'It's my birthday. I'll be twenty. A big girl,' she looked embarrassed and could feel her face reddening. 'I just want to spend it here and home again – from Paris to London and in between – up in the clouds! The end to a fantasy that never was – and damned silly, I suppose?'

'Silly – yes. But okay. If you can get a flight, meet me on Thursday evening, 9th May. I don't have classes on the Friday, presuming that the University is open and that the students will be attending classes again – who knows what we'll be doing – so we could spend the day in Paris, on the Friday, a night together – no two? Get a flight late on Saturday and I'll drive you to Orly airport – on your birthday. We can lunch there – and a bottle of champagne.'

'Shall I leave my things here, rather than cart them into Paris?'

'We can do a detour and come by as we go to the airport. It shouldn't take too long.'

'If I'm not there, it means I've gone earlier. Otherwise, let's do it! That's a promise. *A bientôt mon ami – mon amour.*' She winked, as if it was all a joke, but inside, for her, it was other than that, and she had an overwhelming feeling of sadness.

'That's a promise, little Ella. That is a promise.' He gently pushed her back against the wall and pressed himself against her. 'A promise. Meet me at the hotel in Paris – Avenue de l'Opéra – Thursday, seven o'clock for an apéritif before dinner. I'll be there anyway. Here's the address and phone number, and you can always leave a message at reception.' He tucked a hotel card down beneath the neck of her sweater and let his hand linger against her breast. '*A bientôt*, my little English girl.' This echo of Philippe Gravelin momentarily shocked her, but she grinned, as if continuing a lighthearted exchange of pleasantries.

'*Ah oui, mon professeur. A bientôt!*'

The following Thursday, 9th May, she'd packed her bags and left them in the hall outside her room, ready to be collected on Saturday on her way to the airport. A small suitcase was all she intended to take with her to Paris, and in spite of the dire warnings of how things there were getting out of control, she felt happy at the prospect of leaving this place, and very happy to think towards the intervening few days. She intended to go into Paris early, deposit her suitcase at the left luggage in Saint-Lazare station, amuse herself in the city, then meet Alain at the hotel.

She had told both Madeleine and Madame Vinelli that she would be leaving on Saturday, and each, in her own way, had expressed sorrow and had wished her well. When she'd told them that she would drop by to collect the rest of her things, and that Alain had offered to bring her back and then drive her to the airport, they had nodded and said nothing further.

On Thursday, before she left, Madeleine let her know that she and her mother intended to go through to Rouen to spend the weekend with Sissy and Madame Laval.

'I'll walk down to the station with you,' Madeleine said. 'I want to find out the times of trains to Rouen and check on the connection at Pontoise. You won't need a key, will you? Not if Alain is bringing you over on Saturday. He still has his set of keys.'

Ella wanted so much to ask whether he would be returning to the family home, and whether, in the end, things might turn out alright between them, but the expression on Madeleine's face whenever mention was made of her husband forbade her from doing so.

The two women walked down together to the station at the foot of the hill. Madame Vinelli waved to her from the back door, and as they passed the Fontenay house, Ella looked back at *La Fauvette*, recognizing that this would be the last time she would see it in quite this way. On Saturday she would simply collect her bags and the house would be left empty.

'I haven't said goodbye to Monsieur Charles.' She glanced over to his house.

'He isn't there. I'll tell him that you've left,' and then

Madeleine added – 'he'll be sorry to have missed you. I'm sure that I can pass on his good wishes in his absence.'
Ella nodded. The train was on time. She would not be leaving from this station again. She embraced Madeleine. 'Give Sissy my love, and plenty of big kisses. Tell her I'll miss her. Perhaps one day, when she's a big girl, she'll come and see me in London.'
'Write to us, Ella.'
'Of course.'
She climbed aboard and waved as the train moved out of the station, the long name of Montesson-la-Forêt sliding by into her past.

This might seem to be the end of the story, all but a final few days of happiness, in the spring, in one of the most beautiful of cities: the end of a brief affair and just a stage in Ella's life. But that is not the case, for the real purpose of this tale belongs with what follows, when for a short time a part of the civilized world confronted its demons, and human nature opened to display its hellish interior. For many, the public events which followed would not be forgotten and would be debated over for many, many years to come, but for Ella, a small private event would remain in her memory for ever.

IX

When Ella arrived at the hotel that Thursday evening, there was no sign of Alain Tessier. Feeling slightly disappointed at his not being there to greet her, she accepted the receptionist's invitation to wait for him in the hotel foyer. The sofa there looked out onto a small courtyard, with ornamental trees and a fountain, and she could see into the adjacent restaurant. At first, she contented herself with a comfortable seat after having spent the day walking round Paris, and she slipped off her shoes and leant back against the plush upholstery. For someone who was always short of money, Alain had certainly splashed out on this accommodation. During the day, she had wandered round places she had come to know quite well, walking down from the Opera House to check the whereabouts of the hotel, then on to the Tuileries gardens, visiting old haunts like the Orangerie. She had felt the tension within the city, with news vendors displaying headlines on the current conflict between students, workers and government and, for many, the too hasty intervention by the armed police. Plenty were already critical of the President for his failure to establish calm, and the bourgeoisie were in general becoming increasingly sympathetic towards the young, shocked to hear of the harsh and violent treatment being meted out to them. But all this seemed distant from her, apart from her dreamy contentment. Towards the end of the morning, she'd taken the Métro into the wealthy Sixteenth *arrondissement*, walking to the quiet calm of the Marmottan museum. Mid-afternoon found her sitting in a nearby park, watching the well-dressed children of the rich playing under the supervision of mothers, grandmothers and, most often, nannies, who sat in the warm spring weather, shaded by trees dressed in their brightest green, chatting to each other. Ella thought of Sissy and missed her.

The day had been uneventful and always in her mind was the thought of the evening ahead and the excitement of imagined pleasure. As she'd watched the children playing in the sandpit, climbing on the old 'hygienic horses,' designed to strengthen leg muscles and provide healthy exercise, she had thought over the year and all that had happened since she had quite literally fallen before Alain Tessier.

At a quarter to eight, she went back to the reception desk to see if any message had been handed or phoned in for her. There was nothing. The receptionist had finished for the day, and the night concierge was now on duty. She left her case with him, and he gazed after her, as she went out through the courtyard to the main hotel entrance, his eyes heavy with boredom at the prospect of a long night seated at the desk. There was no sign of Alain in the street. She wandered along the pavement, stopping to look in at the expensive boutiques, jewellery and clothes sparely displayed to suggest exclusivity. They were not the sort of shops which placed price labels, and she amused herself by trying to guess the cost of items. When she returned to the hotel, there had still been no message.

It was eight-fifteen when he finally arrived, and she was surprised and upset to see that he was not alone but was accompanied by Philippe Gravelin. Three young men, obviously students, also followed him in, trooping past the concierge, who looked doubtfully at them and made as if to prevent them from entering.

'It's alright,' Alain explained. 'They're with me. We're going to dine in the restaurant here.' And then, as if an afterthought, 'I have a room reservation – the name of Tessier,' he bent over as the concierge ran his finger down the list of bookings. '*Voilà*,' he directed the man's finger towards his name. 'That's it. You need identification, of course.' He passed over his card and turned towards Ella. 'Ella, you've got your passport?' She went through. The concierge checked the passport as she filled in the obligatory form, shrugged his shoulders and sank back in his chair, muttering something about students to himself and anyone else who might be listening.

'Huh?' said Alain. 'You said something?'

'*Non*. Nothing, nothing. It's students. I mean I've got to be careful. When you hear what they're saying on the radio ... well, you just don't know.'

'It's alright. It's alright. They're with me. No saboteurs! See my papers,' he pulled out a folded paper from his breast pocket. '*Professeur* – at the University. No worries. Relax, relax. Look at him,' he pointed to Philippe Gravelin. 'He's on the administration, part of the secretariat at the Sorbonne. You've no cause to worry.'

The concierge shrugged his shoulders again, lowered his head, but his lips continued to move as if he was talking to himself, reassuring himself.

'Right, come on,' said Alain. '*A table, mes enfants*,' and everyone followed him through to the restaurant beyond. Philippe Gravelin arranged for two tables to be brought together, so that six of them could be accommodated, and it was only when they were all seated that Alain turned to Ella and apologized for his lateness, then immediately introduced her to the three students, Yves, Paul and Robert. There was a feverish atmosphere round the table, and Ella found it hard to plug into this strange energy which seemed to have a momentum of its own. As the evening progressed she began to realize that this was a continuation of the activities of the day, and that the two men and the students had been for hours caught up in the growing agitation in the Latin Quarter, and beyond.

'Well, in my opinion,' said Philippe selecting a variety of shellfish from the huge platter before them, 'the police moved too quickly,' he scooped out the soft morsels and sucked them into his mouth.

Alain reached for an oyster, and Ella watched him as he eased it free from the shell and tipped it onto his tongue. The empty shells clattered into the bowl for the detritus. 'Well they had to block their passage, I know that,' he said, 'but you could see – they should have known that that was only going to aggravate the situation. They're all coming in too heavy, too heavy.'

'Did you see Michel? Did you see him? Huh?' one of the students (Ella thought he was the one called Yves but she wasn't sure) was leaning across the table, brandishing a lobster claw. 'Did you see how that bastard set about him – blood was running down his face and he just pushed him in – like a sack of rubbish – into the Black Maria? Arresting students, imprisoning students, it's firing the anger.'

'Agh! Foul pigs.' The smallest of the three young men took another oyster, leant back and let it slide slowly into his mouth. Philippe picked about for one or two prawns and Ella watched as he beheaded them, pulled off their legs – left the tails – and popped them one after the another into his mouth, crunching the pink shell. She felt tired and less and less hungry.

'Ella! Eat,' said Alain, suddenly turning to her and scooping a couple of oysters onto her plate. 'Who's for more wine?'

As the evening progressed, the conversation became more excitable, more agitated, as back and forth accounts were given of how the day had gone, how it should have gone, how it might have gone, and how things could well be the following day. The rare, red steaks chimed with the talk of injuries they had seen and brutalities witnessed, and like a contrapuntal beat to the rhythm of revolution their knives and forks clattered on the plates. Wine and blood oozed round the table.

'And when they charged like that, across from the Sorbonne, and when they were levering up the cobbles and hurling them ....' Philippe's eyes were wild. He pushed a large piece of steak into his mouth and Ella watched as it churned around between his teeth, a little trickle of blood spilling down his chin. 'And if I get that bastard ...' but what he would do to the bastard, and who the bastard might be, was lost in the mêlée of talk, which began to rise to a crescendo. Other diners glanced across to their table.

Over coffees, and after the students had left, Philippe said that he'd decided not to return to Montesson that night but would, most probably, stay on in an hotel, so that he could get to his office early the following morning when it was expected that the opening of the University might be once again under threat.

'I've got to be around. You can be sure that the police will get there early – they'll have been everywhere all night. I don't know about the gently gently approach you prefer.' He pushed his chair back, threw down the white napkin, and beckoned to the waiter.

In the bedroom, Ella removed the dark blue counterpane from the bed. She'd felt out of it all through the meal. The evening had turned out so very differently from how she'd dreamt it would be. A candlelit romance for two, with sweet seduction, had turned into this feverish jostling of voices accompanied by frenzied absorption of food and drink.

'That was good, good.' Alain lay down on the bed, still fully clothed. 'I hadn't eaten since breakfast – just a coffee, midday, that's all. Exhausting.' He caught sight of her face in the mirror on the wall at the foot of the bed. 'You're not pleased. Forgive me.' He sat up and clutched hold of her skirt. She shook it free. 'You're not going to sulk are you?'

'But you never gave me a thought. You never bothered to think that I would've been waiting for you since seven. That was our time – that was our promise.'

'I did think, but you don't know what it's been like. I went to see Gravelin to find out if he knew anything – I couldn't imagine how on earth anything was going to stem the surge of anger – I'd had those students – and others, I can tell you – petitioning me to do something. Unstoppable is not a meaningless word – the way things are going it's becoming unstoppable. It's both sides, all sides – the police unstoppable, the students unstoppable, the workers – like great tides ....' He saw her incredulous expression. 'Alright. You don't believe me. You think that I just didn't bother to turn up. Alright, but come with me tomorrow. Just come with me and see for yourself.'

By the time Ella emerged from the bathroom, Alain was fast asleep and gently snoring. His clothes were on the chair, and in spite of herself, she smiled to see that drunk as he was, tired as he was, he still had folded them neatly, and his shoes, the socks stuffed inside, were placed side by side at the foot of the bed. She pulled back the blankets, trying not to disturb him, and slipped in beside him. He looked so peaceful, and she spontaneously bent over and kissed his forehead. He grunted, stretched out an arm and pulled her onto him.

In the morning he was as good as his word, taking her with him to the Left Bank. But first, early in the morning, when there was still a silver haze rising over the water, they walked together by the Seine. Even amidst all that was going on, there were men peacefully fishing on the quays. It was quiet.

'Forgiven am I?'
'Sort of, but not quite.'
'Tonight I will be?'
'Perhaps, let's see.'
'I think so. Tonight, Ella, I'll make it up to you. Tonight, the birthday champagne. Tonight, our farewell.'

They paused, now and again, to look down river, holding each other tight.

'If you kiss me like that tonight, I'll forgive you.'
'By the end you'll forgive me anything and everything!'
'Is that a promise? I don't go much for your promises.'
'It's a promise, little English girl.'
'Don't call me that. It reminds me of Philippe Gravelin and I'd rather not be reminded of him.'

He looked at his watch. 'It's time we were in his office. I've got to talk to him.'

'Do we have to?'

'He's alright – bit blunt – crude, I suppose. The hunter in him.'

It proved difficult to get through to the administrative block in the University, and when they did, they couldn't find Philippe. Ella was propelled from place to place, listening to confused strands of fragmented information – Nanterre had opened up to give classes – no, there was massive dissent – a sea of protestors against the imprisonment of students – voices chanting, screaming for their liberation. She desperately tried to keep close to Alain, but was pushed and shoved, verbally and physically, panicking as she was caught in the press of bodies, swaying this way and that with this human mass. The shouting and the screaming of angry voices, the beating of sticks on metal, seemed part of a swollen and furious river.

The day went by with demonstrations, marching protestors, snatched food amidst noise, noise and more noise. Long ago, she'd lost all sense of where she was and what she was doing there. All she wanted was to get out. Twice she'd lost Alain, but each time she'd caught up with him. God knew how! But it wasn't until well into the evening, when they finally met Philippe and went with him to find a small café, one of the few still serving, that she felt some temporary relief. The patron gave them a bowl of stewed lamb and vegetables, but he was anxious and wanted to get rid of them as soon as he could, so that he could close the bar and lock the doors. Ella watched him secure the shutters.

'Can we leave, Alain? Can we get out of here?' and for the first time – 'I'm frightened.'

'Okay, we'll set off.' He shook hands with Philippe, who grinned.

'Leaving the party already. The night's still young,' he

glanced at his watch. Not ten yet,' and kissed Ella on both cheeks. 'Don't like it when it gets rough, Ella?'

'Alain. Get me out!' and her voice came out strangely high-pitched – a shout which alerted the patron.

'What's going on? What's the matter with her?'

'She's sick,' said Philippe. 'Just sick. We'll get her away.'

And that was when it all started. Like a strange signal in her brain as they stepped out into hell. Huge barricades were being erected, overturned cars, torn up railings, piles and piles of cobbles from the narrow roads and pavements, and they ran backwards and forwards like rats in a maze. One way there were students, another, the armed police, black bitter faces beating down violent blows, white batons, black batons, everywhere, on anyone. Big shields and invisible eyes, a pack bearing down and she wanted to curl up on the ground like an animal under attack. The cobblestones, dug up by students, hurled towards the shields of the black and white force, and then the water jets, the thick smell of gas which burned the face and blinded. Ella had lost Alain. Screaming, she was screaming, running this way and that. A blow caught her heavily on the shoulder. Then she saw him, carrying a girl, her eyes closed, her head hanging over his arm and blood dripping from a wound on the top of her head. She saw him shouting to be let past, and she ran to him. 'Help me! Help me!'

'This girl. Let me through. Ella, clear a way through.' And amazingly, just for a moment, the sea parted and they reached a shrieking ambulance. Ella shrank back as she saw a young man lying on the ground and a helmeted policeman beating him, again and again and again, on the head, on the arm, on the leg, on the back, and kicking him in a frenzy of attack.

'Stop it! Stop it!' and he turned to her, raising the baton towards her. Alain pulling her away. And then the fires. The cars alight, burning furiously, leaping flames, explosions as another and another fuel tank caught. The Molotov cocktails, spasmodic bursts of fire. The gas, the air blue and bitter tasting. She turned and her eyes were wide as she saw these strange white-faced people coming towards her – faces covered with white powder, some with damp and clinging handkerchiefs over their faces – it was like a strange ballet, seeming to go slow, slow, slow. Her eyes stinging, she was fainting, she was falling, going thinner and thinner and away from it all.

The force of the water jet caught her on the back and sent her sprawling – winded. And there, Alain, she could see him, ahead of her, down a small alley, against the wall – and Philippe Gravelin. At last, when she'd thought she'd lost them forever. Her legs felt heavy, great things that wouldn't move, and they were bleeding and she didn't know where the wounds had come from. She tried to move towards them.

Stopped.   What?   What?   What?

The assailant was raining down blow upon blow on the head of a man. And the man was trying to cover himself with his hands, scratching scrabbling flailing about to protect himself and to get away from the force of these blows and the hurt. The assailant was using a large iron railing and the blood poured down the man until he fell like a heavy soft object, like a bag of old washing, until he lay there shaking like an electric thing, a thing which was still being beaten until it became quite still, quite, quite still and didn't move anymore. And the assailant was Philippe Gravelin and the beaten man, the man who was dead, was Alain Tessier and the person watching was Ella and she was swept away in the sea and on and on until she finally found herself out in a bay, where there was open space and room to breathe and where she had no idea where she was and who she was and what she had seen.

It was Saturday, and Ella was leaving the hotel on the Avenue de l'Opéra. She had settled the bill, had explained that Monsieur Tessier would not be returning and that she was taking his small bag for him – should he ask – but he would not ask. She was walking down the Avenue, as she had done so many times in the past, and heading towards the terrible debris of the night before. She had not slept, having arrived at the hotel past midnight, beating on the glass entrance door, screaming to be let in. The concierge had been asleep at his desk, had refused her entrance, failed to recognize that she was the same young woman from the evening before, had eventually let her in, taken her to her room – left her. It had been hours before she had begun to examine what had taken place, hours before she could undress, bathe, and piece herself together and some, but not all, of the events of this dreadful night. Still she could not turn a part of her mind towards what she had witnessed; still it was as if a wall divided off a section of her brain, refusing to allow her imagination in to see again a horror for which she had no translation into comprehensible language. The appalling terror remained sealed, and as she watched the room gradually grow lighter, and as she looked out through the window, holding back the muslin curtain, slowly, slowly she faced another interior window of her own, where the face of Alain Tessier gazed sorrowfully out into a similarly empty environment.

When she reached the scenes of the previous night's violence, she saw the way ahead jagged with overturned cars, heaps of broken glass, cobblestones piled high and supported by metal ripped from railings and grids, anything and everything, to form the barricades. Trees had been felled and their branches strewn like torn limbs. Carefully, she stepped and climbed over the carnage, crawling over blockages, oblivious to the graffiti and the blank staring faces of others who wandered through this nightmare, dazed by what had happened. Riot police stood around like pieces of flotsam which had broken away from the huge black ferocity of the night before. She was seeking that alleyway.

'Do you want something, *Mademoiselle*? You can't come by here. This street is closed.' A policeman, still in riot gear, took her arm and led her away. 'Have you lost something?'

'Yes.'

'You can report it,' he looked around at the burnt-out carcasses of cars. 'Is it your car? Has your car been taken?'

'No not my car. I've lost someone.'

'Ah! Well plenty of people lost somebody, last night.' And she was surprised to hear him laugh. 'Scattered students – all over the place. Sleeping it off anywhere they can find, ready for the next onslaught – and your friend – boyfriend? – he'll be as lost as you.'

'He's dead.'

He looked at her strange face. 'I don't think so. Wounded. You need the hospital. They're compiling a list of the wounded and ones arrested, and there are plenty of those. There'll be a list. Give them time. There's always a list.'

'He's dead. Clubbed to death.'

'I don't think so,' and now his voice was hard, no longer sympathetic. 'Are you making some complaint against the police? That what it's about?' His fingers clenched round her arm as he pushed her forwards. She tripped over one of the large uprooted cobblestones and almost fell. 'Come on, get on with you. On your way. On your way.' He directed her towards the police *commissariat*, where, he said, she might be more able to gain information. 'I tell you, though – and be warned – they'll not want to hear about your complaints, no more do I. That's what it is, is it? I'd get on your way, girl, just get on your way and out of our hair.'

Instead of any police station or hospital, she went to the station of Saint-Lazare: a small figure, maroon suitcase in one hand, clutching a soft, brown leather bag to her breast with the other. The trains were running, the concourse busy. She had a desperate need to get away – out of it all. She didn't know where to turn and whom to tell. The police didn't want to know. Somebody being beaten, *Mademoiselle*? Tell me news! So many beaten, so many injured. Somebody dead? Get out of it! You a relative? Just a friend. How could she tell Madeleine and Madame Vinelli? Philippe Gravelin was someone close to them, well respected, and a firm friend of Alain Tessier. He was from a local family who had lived in Montesson for years. What are you talking about, little English girl? She saw the closing of doors upon an outsider – a foreigner from over the water. She stared out of the carriage window as the familiar names of each station appeared. At Montesson-la-Forêt she got out and, as if walking in her sleep, set off, once more, through the tunnel beneath the track, across the road to Paris, up the hill towards *La Fauvette*.

She didn't have a key, and she remembered, dimly, that the two women had gone to Rouen, and that she was supposed to be arriving here by car with Alain, and that the keys would be in his pocket with his identity card. Even now, someone would be looking through his possessions, itemizing them: wallet one; set of keys two; photograph of a little girl one. Name? Address? Place of work?

Automatically, she went to see if that small window was open, but she knew it would be, because it was never closed – the stench, you see, it was the stench. She pushed her case into the bushes of hortensias, intending to collect it later, and still hugging the soft, brown bag, she climbed, as she had done before, onto the dustbin and slid through the small window. Her shoulder bag, which she'd hooked round her neck, caught on the window catch and pulled tight at her throat, so that, for a moment, she was hanging there, feet dangling over the lavatory pan.

All her belongings were still piled neatly outside her bedroom door, just as she had left them. She walked through the hall, past Madame Vinelli's bedroom, towards the cases, and heard a loud exclamation from the room opposite her bedroom. She stood still. The door to the sitting-room was open a few inches. She pressed herself back against the wall as she heard Philippe Gravelin's voice, speaking earnestly, strongly, loudly.

'That's right. What you wanted. Done. And now?'

There was a long silence. Who was he talking to? Ella was barely breathing, terrified of making any noise.

'Now don't act the little girl. Don't give me that. You know what you wanted.'

There was a sound of another voice, but it was so soft that Ella couldn't make out the words.

'I said, don't give me that.'

'It's not true. That's not what I want at all. I don't want that at all. Go away! Go away! Leave me alone.' It was Madeleine. Why wasn't she in Rouen?

'Oh, dear, dear. Not what you wanted. Don't upset me. You know very well what you wanted.'

'Not true.'

'What's not true? You think he's not dead? I do the work and you reap the benefits? Listen *ma petite* - no don't you walk away' - Ella held her breath as she heard his voice move closer to the door - 'don't think you can change your mind when it doesn't suit anymore.' There was a strange yelping sound. 'You can cry as much as you like.'

'Get out! Get out!' The voice was momentarily less distinct, as if Madeleine was pacing back and forwards. She was saying something about the police and justice. '... get away with murder.'

He laughed, a great guffaw. 'You silly girl. I've got all your letters to old Fontenay. You've made it perfectly clear that you wanted your husband out of the way. Believe me, if I go down, you come with me. Madame

118

Vinelli, Marguerite? All her little secrets! I should keep quiet if I were you.'
'It's not true. Not true.'
'Don't keep on. You're wearying me. You're getting me down.'
'I never said that. Never. Not that. I didn't – I didn't. It's not true. It's a lie.'
'A lie, is it? You accusing me of lying? Now, now. Let's not have this.'
'No don't. Please. Please.'
'I'm a hunter, girl.' Ella heard a scuffle and then a heavy thud. She held her breath. There was a crash of glass. 'Now look what you've done. I want you, Madeleine. I want you. I've waited a long, long time for this. I've been prepared to wait.'
'Don't! Don't touch me.'
'Now look, little girl, I'm getting a bit tired of all this. You think I'm lying? No. No.' There was a silence, then what sounded like a rustle of paper. 'I couldn't get the ring off. I thought you'd want to see it – make sure, you know, like know for certain – have the proof. I cut the finger off, all of it – had to. I didn't want to – it complicates …'

Madeleine's scream filled the house. Ella jumped, quite literally jumped with fear. Back across the hall – quiet – quiet. Couldn't risk the door, not the big key that squeaked – the small window – impossible the other way, not without a noise – the cellar – bolts never shot – Shot! Shot! Shot! – guns and Gravelin – no – down the steps – the door to the garden let it be open, please God, this once, let it be open, again, again, as it often is – not shut from the outside.

Open! Open! Thank heaven! Light and fresh gust of air and the morning sun. But not over yet. Keeping close to the wall, beneath the window, round the side of the house and run, run, down to the road. Can't wait for a train. A car. Please stop! Please stop! Yes. Could you – Paris? Please?

The car pulled to a halt a little further up the road, and a man leant out. 'Can I help you, *Mademoiselle*?'

She cleared her throat, and very calmly said – 'I need to get to Paris.'

'Paris! It's not the best place to be today. Haven't you heard the news? Rioting. It was all broadcast on the radio. Terrible fighting. God knows!'

'I didn't know. I've got to get a train to the airport. I've a plane to catch this evening. I mean, if you're going to Paris, or perhaps drop me nearby and I'll try for a train? I mean, Argenteuil, that would do. Just away from here. That's all.'

He stared at her, clearly puzzled. 'Look, if you want, I'll take you to the airport. If it's Orly?'

'Of course not. I wouldn't dream of ...'

'I was going into Paris – I was supposed to be working, but I've been in two minds about it. I don't want to get caught up in the riots – it's starting again. And if I don't go to work – the day's my own. I'll go and watch the planes myself. Have a day out. Play hooky! Go on, jump in.'

And she did. Still holding that small, soft leather bag against her heart, she arrived at Orly and later boarded her plane. All she had with her were the clothes she stood up in, her small shoulder bag, containing passport, money and plane ticket. In the soft bag were Alain's night things and a few papers, including lecture notes on the theory of revolution and a slim copy of his final novel: *Betrayal*.

The plane soared into the clouds but a little later they thinned and she saw the last of the French coast. She never returned to Paris and nobody came looking for her.

One day, much, much later, she took that small brown bag and threw it, with all her force, into the Thames.

X

In July 1998, thirty years after what are now known in France as *Les Evénements* – the Events of 1968 – and elsewhere as the near revolution, for some the most sensational of all the tumult across Europe, north America and beyond, a woman was drinking iced lemonade in the French ski resort of Chamonix. Reading *Le Figaro*, she occasionally glanced up into the bright sunshine at the snow-capped peak of Mont Blanc. A book on the table beside her was English, and when she called over to the waiter to ask for the bill, it was clear from her accent that she was not French, so presumably English. Her name was Ella Rush, and thirty years before she had been in Paris at the time of those 'Events.' Around her now French patriots were still celebrating their winning of the World Cup, and from time to time, young voices continued the chants that had filled the streets the night before: '*Champions du Monde!*' – 'World Champions!'

The woman smiled, paid her bill, but remained seated at the table, her eye having been caught by an article in the newspaper. Musing on the winning of the cup and the surge of patriotic fervour, the journalist was reflecting upon the way in which great collective movements can rise directly from the people, seemingly having nothing to do with government directives. He wrote of the fall of the Berlin Wall, the implosion of communism, the mass emotion of the previous year, at the death of Princess Diana – and then, the force of the 1968 riots. The woman closed her eyes, as she, too, recalled that uprising which, in its ferocity, flashed fear across Europe, and then died almost, so it was said, as quickly as it had begun: like a spontaneous combustion which had burnt itself out – like a fish, gold – catching the sparkle of the sun – falling from the sky. Why did she think of that? She placed her head on one side and tapped a finger against the glass on the table. Why did she think of that? Another memory returned, and with this an image which had barely dimmed for her. She picked up her bag – and the newspaper, but then, shrugging her shoulders, placed that down on the chair. She'd rather not have the reminder. Was it thirty years ago? How strange that she had not realized, even though she had certainly not forgotten those 'Events' and, for her, their personal significance.

It was an impulse which took her off, away from the Alps, across France, driving north-westwards towards Paris. It was hot in the car, and she frequently stopped en route, staying one or two nights, sometimes longer, at small hotels, making the most of her holiday. She took a week over the journey, arriving at last at a small village on the west of Paris called Montesson-la-Forêt. She parked her car down by the Seine and walked up in the direction of the forest, pausing after a little way to read the name, Monsieur Charles Fontenay, on the mailbox outside a large house concealed behind huge overgrown trees. A little further up, on the left, she found a small tarmacadamed road, rue J-J Rousseau, and not far along this neat road, she saw an old rendered building, the rendering grey and flaking. She stopped by the mailbox and read that this was the home of Monsieur and Madame Philippe Gravelin. Returning down the road, she visited the small station, and planned to leave, but at the front of the station, a very old man was selling bunches of wild roses. His legs were bandaged and he sat beside a stick. She picked up a bunch and handed him a few francs, and then, instead of going back to her car, as she had intended, she retraced her steps up the hill, back towards the grey house called *La Fauvette*.

She hesitated at the entrance to the house, and an alsatian started to bark in the garden next door, flinging itself against the wire netting with such force that she thought it would surely burst through. A neighbour came out to silence the dog, and seeing the stranger asked if she needed assistance.

'I was just wondering whether Madame Tessier still lived here?'

'Tessier? No. Gravelin.'

'Oh, I'm so sorry. I've obviously made a mistake.'

'That's alright.'

'I spent a little time here when Madame Vinelli ...'

'Ah Madame Vinelli! Well, of course, she died some years ago, and it's her daughter who lives here, married to Monsieur Gravelin. I believe she was married before, though. Yes – her husband died.'

'I see. Thank you so much.'

Holding her bunch of red roses, she went round the house to the front door. The porch was clean and the door clearly used. She rang the bell and a woman, rather overweight and dark-haired, opened the door.

'I'm sorry to bother you, I'm looking for Madame Madeleine Tessier.'

The woman at first did not respond and Ella thought that she was going to close the door. 'Madame Gravelin, Madame Madeleine Gravelin,' she finally said. 'But – my name was Tessier.'

'I'm sure you won't remember me, but I looked after your little girl, Sissy, for a few months, a long time ago. I'm from England. My name's Ella Rush.'

'Ella Rush?' she looked puzzled, but then her face cleared. 'Oh, yes, of course. You looked after Simone! Of course. Indeed, I remember. Do come in. Philippe!' she called up the stairs. She noticed that Ella was taking off her thin jacket. 'Let me put that in the bedroom for you.'

Ella held out the bunch of red roses. 'For you, Madame.'

'How kind.' Ella followed her towards what had been Madame Vinelli's room. The other woman lay Ella's little jacket on the white bedspread, and put the roses down there, too. 'I'll put them in water in a minute. Do come through to the salon next door. How nice to see you! I'll tell Simone that you called. She's married now with children of her own.'

Ella noticed how changed the bedroom was. It was clearly occupied now by Madeleine and Philippe. She heard footsteps in the hall behind, and turned to greet an elderly man, tall and still recognizable as Philippe Gravelin. He held out his hand, and, feeling a strange coldness inside her, she took it in her own.

'*Bonjour Monsieur.* You'll not remember who I am, I'm sure.'

Madame Gravelin explained, and he roared with laughter. 'Ah! The little English girl. Good God!'

Over a coffee and a little liqueur, the two of them explained that Alain Tessier, whom she would remember, of course (did Ella catch a knowing glint in the eyes of each? She wasn't sure) had died many years ago. It had been during the riots in Paris. Ella nodded. She, Madeleine Tessier, had married Monsieur Gravelin the same year. Ella was directed towards a small shrine in the corner of the room.

'My late husband was a martyr for the cause,' she lowered her voice. 'Many young people come to visit to pay their respects. He died for them.'

Ella went over to the shrine. There was a photograph of Alain, a small candle, fresh flowers. On a shelf beneath were arranged examples of his writings, published political essays and slim volumes of fiction. She leant over and touched one entitled *Betrayal*.

'Yes,' said Madame Gravelin, coming up behind her to see what had caught her attention. 'That was his last book. He'd just received the final print from the publisher when he died.' She lowered her voice. 'Killed.'

Ella turned round and looked at Monsieur Gravelin, but he seemed to be preoccupied with his pipe, or perhaps he hadn't heard.

'Killed?' she said.

'Oh yes. This is not the official version, but it is the one that's true. He supported the students in their protest, many aspects of their protest, and it was during the rioting that he was battered to death by the riot police.'

Again Ella looked towards Monsieur Gravelin, but he was leaning back in his chair and appeared lost in thought, gently exhaling wreaths of tobacco smoke.

'It was extraordinary. My husband, I mean Philippe, had tried to protect him, and it was he who took his body to the hospital – but of course he was dead – and the police begged him, and begged me, to accept it as accidental death, a coronary. They were terrified that news of any death, and at the hands of the police, would provoke further violence – civil war, you know – they said it was a possibility. The President left the country to gather military strength – that's what they said. We agreed to hush it up.'

Ella nodded, acknowledging the magnanimity of such a gesture.

'We keep the shrine.' This was Philippe Gravelin's voice.

'And Monsieur Fontenay? I passed his house on the way here.'

Madame looked away, and just for a moment she seemed confused. 'Him!' she finally answered. 'He's quite a celebrity, you know. He owns that house, still, but it's Paris now and only the best. Haven't you seen the film based on his latest book? You must. You must.'

When Ella got up to go, she thanked them both for their hospitality. 'Please, I'll get my jacket.' She signalled to Madeleine not to bother, she knew the way to the bedroom. For a moment, she stood alone in the hall. The old W.C. must have been modernized, for there was a new door and a strong scent of lavender. She glanced up the stairs. All history now, but soon to be a past ready to be dug up and sifted through: last March she'd read that the usual fifty-year seal upon the opening of 1968 archived material was to be waived and access allowed.

Already the metaphorical skeletons were beginning to rattle their bones.

She went into Madame Vinelli's old room, and as she slipped on the jacket, she glanced down at the roses, still lying there. The bright red of the petals was vivid against the white. But even as she looked, she saw lines of ants, so many of them, seeping out from within the flowers like dark runnels of dirt spreading across the marital bed.